Lord Lister, known as Raffles, Master Thief

Novel No. 3

The Royal Palace Medal Robbery

by Kurt Matull

translated by Joseph A. Lovece

Dime Novel Cover Vol. 17

ISBN-13: 9798709881136

Also by the author:

The Steam Man of the West
The Road Home
The Flying Prairie Schooner
The Transatlantic Race
The Tablet of Destiny
Juan Nadie

Dime Novel Robots1868-1899: An Illustrated History and
Bibliography

Dime Novel Cover:

Denver Doll the Detective Queen
Six Weeks in the Moon
Hank Hound, the Crescent City Detective
Sherlock Holmes Versus Jack the Ripper
Hercules, the Dumb Destroyer
Night Hawk
Sexton Blake: The Missing Millionaire
Lord Lister Known as Raffles, Master Thief
Fantastic, Amazing and Beautiful Dime Novel Art
European Dime Novel Art
Ripping and Cracking, Penny Dreadful and Boys' Weekly Art
The Witch Hunter's Wards
The James Boys and Pinkerton
Harry Dickson the American Sherlock Holmes
Jörn Farrow's U-Boat Adventures: The Sea Monster
Sexton Blake: A Christmas Crime
The Silent City
Lord Lister 2: The Fake Jeweler's Punishment

Penny Dreadful Press

Claude Duval: The Sword of Vengeance
Spring-Heeled Jack: Man or Fiend

Preface

With the third Lord Lister novel his actions get increasingly daring and the social criticism heats up. Even his assistant the skittish Charlie Brand grows increasingly bold, wearing disguises and engaging the targets.

Here the author Kurt Matull directly takes aim at slices of the British aristocracy. In particular, the book mocks the use of regalia, notably badges, medals, stars, sashes and bands or garters. The German writer did his research and correctly described many of the royal accoutrements England still uses today but seem increasing anachronistic.

Leading the pack is the so-called Most Noble Order of the Garter, one of the highest knighthood levels, outranked only by the Victoria Cross and George Cross. Members are known for their blue sashes and ornate knee bands. In the story the group is disgraced by its younger members, protected by their royal families. Its so-called *femerichter* or in English kangaroo court (an arcane term Germans no longer use, presenting challenges to modern translators) harkens back to medieval torture courts, also a favorite dime novel scenario.

In a society trained to revere and guard the aristocracy such royal symbols are get-out-of-jail cards and passports to every club in town. Lord Lister, always thinking out of the box, or in this case the safe, shamelessly exploits the social blind spot to help those oppressed by the monarchical system. And he does it just for fun and on a whim. The robbery of the royal palace, although profitable, serves Lister no higher purpose other than an entertaining challenge and an opportunity to expand his reputation.

And the psychological torture of Inspector Baxter is icing on the cake.

This translation is from the original 1908 German novel "Der Ordensraub im Königsschlosse". Like every Lister story, this novelette has never been translated into English.

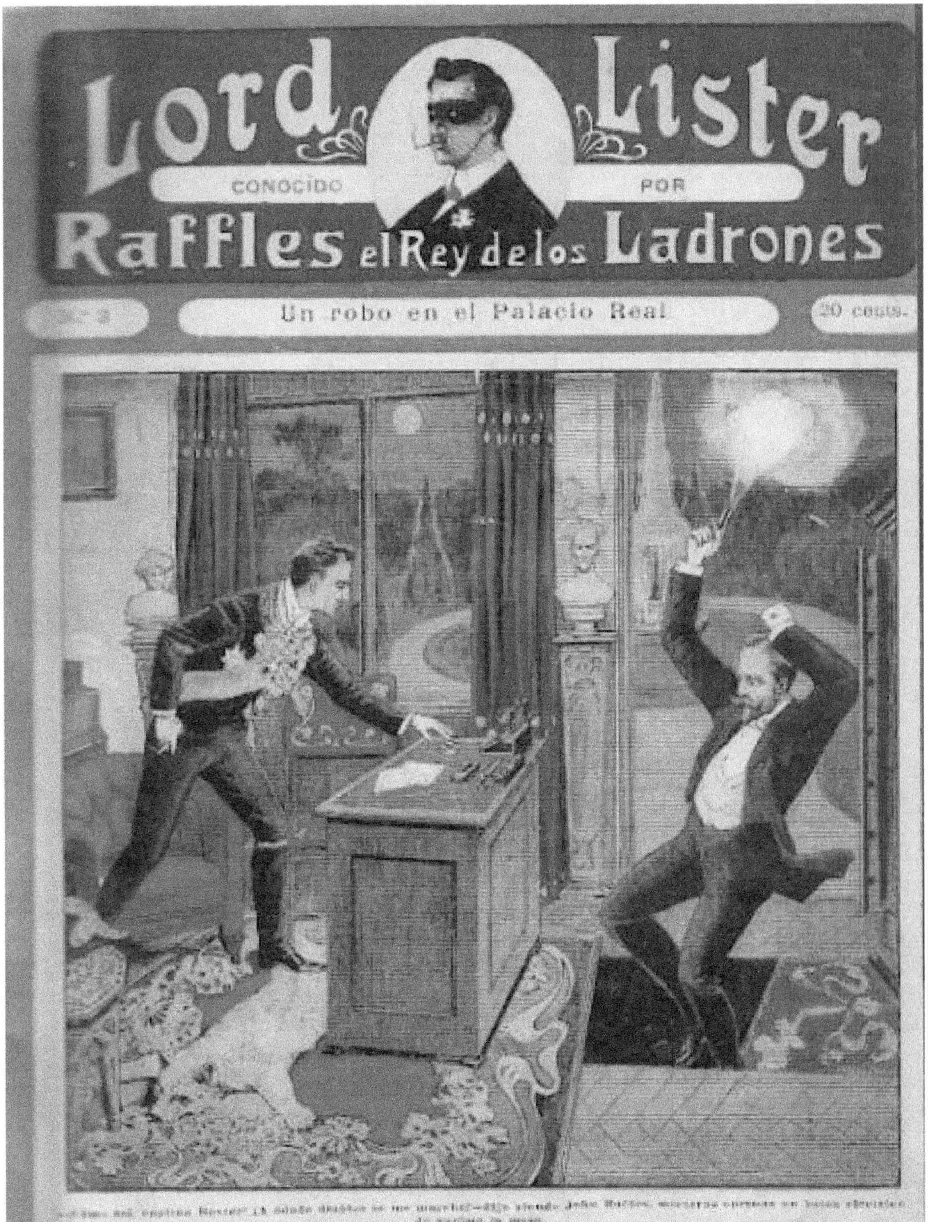
Lord Lister
CONOCIDO POR
Raffles el Rey de los Ladrones
Un robo en el Palacio Real
20 cents.

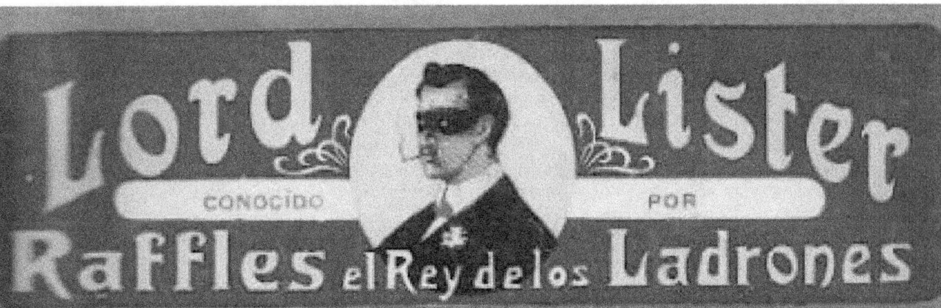

Chapter I

Constable White

At Scotland Yard Constable White arriving in the company of a young woman gave Inspector Baxter his report.

"This young lady," he said, blanching, anxiously pointing to a beautiful girl wearing a veil trying to conceal her face from prying eyes and occasionally police officers, "was pursued by several gentlemen. I managed only with great cunning to evade one of them who apparently believed he was the Lord of London and was completely innocent."

"You must unlearn presenting your reports in such a tone," said the inspector, frowning. Then he turned to the young lady.

"What is your name?"

"My name is Ellen Crofton, sir."

"Good. And where do you live?"

"In Bromley," she answered. The inspector nodded, jotted down the address which she said hesitantly, and muttered to himself:

"What good comes from Bromley?" Then turning back to the questionee he asked, "What does your father do?"

"He was an officer in the Indian Army but left them and has operated a business for some years."

"So you are poor?" said the inspector with brutal instance, while he tried to observe under the veil the young girl's features.

She blushed deeply at the question but nodded her head silently. Inspector Baxter turned back to the constable and said:

"Proceed, constable, what happened?"

White was about to answer when his left arm protested. From a deep flesh wound seeped blood, which had already stained his uniform.

"I was going down St. James Street," explained White, "as this road falls within my jurisdiction."

"One of our most prestigious streets," interrupted the inspector, nodding his head with a troubled expression. "And then?"

"Suddenly I heard cries for help," continued the constable. "I went towards the screams. All of a sudden a house door was violently thrown open and this young lady rushed out, as if in fear of her life, and hurried down the road. The darkness favored her pursuers. There were about six to eight gentlemen—if these guys deserve to be called such, inspector."

"Leave off those remarks," said the officer. "Only distinguished people live in St. James Street; they certainly were members of one of the fashionable clubs."

"That is my conviction, inspector," said Constable White without batting an eye. "These rogues also—"

"Did I not just explain that you will not speak of the St. James Street inhabitants in that tone?" the inspector again interrupted.

"Now then, these strange gentlemen chased her down the street, seized the young woman who had escaped them, jumped on her, one of them covered her mouth to prevent her from screaming, then dragged her back in the direction of the house. I rushed in and ordered them to release her. The wretches, excuse me, the gentlemen, replied with cheeky laughter, so I make short work of two of them, knocking them to the ground and releasing the young lady, threw three of them against a wall, and chased off the other two.

"One of the guys, excuse me, gentlemen, stuck a knife into my arm and he got away."

"And where was the building in which this scene took place?" Baxter asked while walking up and down restlessly, throwing the constable and the young woman disapproving looks.

"It was No. 39 St. James Street."

The address made Baxter nervous, and he looked around and wrung his hands.

"Dammed!" he blurted out. "There are three clubs, three of the most prestigious clubs in London, one even belongs to a royal prince, and you have acted in a most egregious manner against these gentlemen, constable."

White answered:

"But I tell you that these bandits..."

"You are suspended for a day!" replied the inspector angrily. "Don't you know that it's required that in all circumstances you have to know the lay of the land? Who knows what this was about! You interfered in a matter that was not police business."

"When more than a half a dozen men pounce on a single woman it is a police affair," Constable White replied defiantly.

The inspector turned to the young lady who had until then listened in silence.

"How did you get into the clubhouse, miss?"

"I don't know," she said.

The inspector laughed grimly.

"That kind of answer won't cut it with me, lady. Tell me how you got into that house and your relationship with those gentlemen."

"I went for a walk this afternoon in Hyde Park," she said, looking anxiously at the police inspector and glancing at

Constable White as if looking for help. "It was dusk when at a bench I suddenly lost consciousness. When I came to my senses I saw that I was in a house surrounded by a crowd of unknown men, who did not hesitate to assault me. I pushed them aside and ran away. The constable has told you the rest."

"And you think I'm going to buy this story, lady?"

"It's not a story," said the young woman, as she proudly straightened herself up. "If you believe that being an inspector means insulting a defenseless girl, then Col. Crofton will know how to handle you."

"I answer to no colonels," the inspector replied haughtily, "if you are put off, lady. But I'll give you some good advice: from now on don't provoke such affairs and be aware that the police are not here to help you get your life under control."

The constable saw the young lady's face become deathly pale. She uttered a low moan and staggered and would certainly have fallen to the ground had White not caught and supported her.

"Go now," he whispered to her. "Go away from the guardians of the law and have nothing more to do with the police."

She thankfully pressed his hand. Constable White whistled for a car, and a minute later Miss Crofton was gone.

The inspector paced the room like a lion. There was no doubt concerning his anger toward the constable. Suddenly it dawned on the inspector:

"Remember, Constable White, you have only been in the service half a year! You're a newbie! You believe violence is the answer and play by the book. First of all, you have places like St. James Street, Pall Mall, Regent Street, etc. Be less authoritative. Do you understand me? In those posh London neighborhoods you have to exercise some restraint. And if you run in in every time a woman screams, and you'll find that ninety times out of a hundred it's purely a private matter, you'll pull tabs the size of Westminster Abbey's towers.

"You can learn a lot from us, constable. The small, private affairs of the noble class do not concern us. If it is a crime, well, that's different!"

"Is it a crime, inspector, when a group violently attacks a young woman?"

"You're an idiot, constable!"

"Thanks, inspector. And the mysterious matter that the young woman related? Should it not be investigated how Miss Crofton suddenly awoke in the clubhouse?"

"Let's see if her father files a complaint," said the inspector. "Shall we burn our fingers? There's probably some dubious love affair behind the whole story, and the disgraced party would be someone close, say in Scotland Yard."

Constable Baxter turned away with a shrug.

At that moment the telephone rang. A desk sergeant talked on it for a long time, then turned to the inspector:

"Sir Johnathan Woorman asks for special protection, Inspector."

"Sir Woorman? The wealthy Irish landowner? Well, I'll go with a few men. What's the reason for his sudden anxiety?"

"He fears his safe will be robbed, Inspector."

"Right now? And why?"

"Raffles has been seen in the area."

"Raffles? Raffles? Is it really Raffles? Young man, I am on the case! I'll pay a pound note to each of you when we finally get the Great Unknown under our fingers. Goddamn! The guy is driving me crazy!"

"He's said it so many times it could soon be true," murmured Constable White.

Inspector Baxter choose five men besides White, whom he liked for his courage and coolness and because he was available, and they went on their way. The sergeant relayed the orders and the array followed Sir Woorman's cry for help.

"I already have a lot of notes from him," said Baxter on their way. "It seems that he has powerful personal enemies, as he's constantly sending me threatening letters he has received. There have already been two attempts on his person. He's a perfect gentleman, and the only thing one can say about him is the fact that he fancies himself as a Don Juan."

"That's not a crime," laughed the sergeant.

"It depends," White replied softly, but so that the inspector heard it. He turned around instantly and asked, eyeing

White sharply:

"How so, constable? Does the wealthy gentleman's amusements violate your moral principles? You are a strange person, I must say."

"They slum," replied White. "My views are elastic as rubber. But I am of the opinion that distinguished gentlemen should amuse themselves where they belong, namely in their own circles. Instead they seek out their victims where poverty and misery are already inflicting damage."

The inspector laughed loudly, which resonated with the other officers.

"So he should only go with daughters of trade council members or stateroom lords, constable? You are a child! This thing, although you are a competent police officer, is outside of your experience. But we are on the spot."

It was about eleven o'clock at night. Inspector Baxter and his officers entered the sprawling, exuberant and beautifully furnished apartment of Sir Johnathan Woorman, one of London's best-known sportsmen, who enjoyed no small reputation in the highest circles for his perverse pleasures.

Sir Woorman invited them inside.

"Thank you, Inspector, for coming," he said in a squeaky voice which Constable White noticed. He was a tall, broad-shouldered man, but moved gracefully and had a figure which delighted the London ladies. On a fairly long neck sat a vigorously built head, with broad, somewhat blunt features typical of Irishmen.

But for Sir Woorman's elegant attire and manners, which were that of an accomplished cavalier, one might mistake him for a member of the general population.

At least those were the thoughts of Constable White, a police officer who always thought differently from his colleagues.

"Thank you, inspector. What an adventure I had a few hours ago!" said Woorman.

"At least a gallant one," said Baxter.

"The devil take all gallant adventures," said Sir Woorman, who suddenly seemed to have changed his taste. "Thank you, Inspector. Tonight—it was eight o'clock—I had a rendezvous in a small wine restaurant. What kind of restaurant it was doesn't matter. Small, pretty, nice, ideal for little adventures. I'm a friend of it. So I step in, sit down in a small booth, where I wait for the lady—and five minutes later a man walks in to see me. He's very elegant, by the way, your Raffles! So elegant! And cheeky—nothing beats it!"

"Raffles came instead of the lady?" said the inspector. "In the devil's name, how is that possible?"

"If I knew that, inspector, why would I need you?"

"And you're sure it was Raffles? Raffles and no other?"

"It was him. you can rely on it! The guy gave me a big lecture and finally explained to me that I was a—well, that doesn't matter. In any case, he told me that he would take my money tonight, because he was convinced that firstly I had a lot and secondly that it belonged to others. Well, do you have logic for him, then? Simply great! Well, I told him then that I already knew the means to rap his knuckles. I said, 'They'll look for you for a long time, my boy.'"

"And what did he say to that?"

"He put you in a certain category in the zoo. As I said, he is of golden insolence. Well, I think we'll get rid of him putting his hand in my money box, don't you think? I have the greatest confidence in you."

"I will justify your assumption in every way," replied the inspector, both eager and submissive. "I will immediately distribute my people on the stairs and exits and cover all the house entrances."

"So? But then he has the habit of many of his fellow men."

"But not the common burglars," said Inspector Baxter. "You, Sir Woorman, may have the good fortune to guard the room in which your safe is. I will give you Constable White, who is ever so energetic and courageous."

Sir Woorman looked at Constable White, to whom the inspector had pointed with his hand.

"Hm. I like the man. May be very useful! But unfortunately I don't have the time! An urgent request, inspector—but I'm sure your constable can keep watch up here alone!"

"As you wish, Sir Woorman. In this case I myself will sit down with White in the room housing your safe."

"All right!" countered the gentleman. "Incidentally, you should stay in the anteroom because from there you have the best view," replied Sir Woorman. Then he ushered the two officials into the rooms in question, while the other constables occupied the stairs and entrances.

The safe was in a small chamber with two doors. And you could not go up the stairs without a constable hearing it. When they ensconced themselves in the anteroom both Inspector Baxter and White surveyed the second entrance, being in Sir Woorman's empty office.

"Here are cigars and cigarettes," said Sir Woorman, "have a good time, gentlemen! I'll come home tomorrow morning, and by then, hey, all the danger will be over."

"And if the devil doesn't have his hand on the scale again, we will have Raffles, which is worth more to us than ten such safes, Sir Woorman," said the inspector.

It became quiet in the house. Sir Woorman was gone, and Inspector Baxter and Constable White were in the study.

Both took turns watching the safe. In the door there was a large pane of glass through which one could look without difficulty. Also advantageous was that the room with the safe was lit up as bright as day, while the two men looked on in the dark.

"I'll let myself be hung up if Raffles comes up with an cunning plan this time!" said Baxter. "He can't just wave a magic wand and steal even a penny from right before our eyes. It's out of the question."

White didn't answer. While Baxter took a position near the door and did not turn his face for a moment from the brightly lit adjoining room, White had left silently and was now patrolling thoughtfully, a bright lantern on his belt, through the individual rooms of the apartment. Everywhere he stopped he searched with knowledgeable eyes.

"That could be it alright," he mumbled. "Because the safe is completely empty, that's for sure." Without changing his face, Constable White began to open using a small lockpick a wooden panel that looked quite ordinary from the outside. He had hardly removed the wooden door when the light shone on a large armored plate.

After various attempts to open it with a lockpick, White reached for a so-called cutting torch. This instrument was sixty centimeters long and contained in the special device a quantity of gas to ignite the burner's mouth and emit an immensely hot flame. The mixture of oxygen and acetylene contained in the tool produced a temperature of more than seven thousand degrees Celsius. The pressure of the oxygen leaving the combustion tube was about sixteen atmospheres. The resulting blowing effect was enormous under this strong pressure; as the oxygen was drawn from the space already made white-hot by the gas mixture it melted the burning, slushy iron effectively.

Even the best armor plate couldn't withstand such a terrible temperature. It was a proprietary procedure, which Raffles had used several times before, and Constable White used at that moment to melt through the safe.

After five minutes his work was done. The box lay open in front of him, and with indifference, as if the matter were none of his business, Constable White reached inside and emptied the contents of the safe.

There was about £5,000 in there. White put back a hundred pounds, put the rest in his inner breast pocket, and with the light of his lantern studied a large box of letters that had been hidden between the banknotes.

This contained a lover's farewell letter and a newspaper clipping on which an advertisement was circled in red pen.

Shaking his head White looked at the two items. Then he saw that the letter had a trace of blood on it. Again he read the ad:

We are committed to running all varieties of errands and ask you to honor us with future orders; you won't be sorry. Alice Forester and her son, Gerard St, London N.

Constable White shrugged his shoulders and slipped them into his breast pocket. Then he calmly went back to Sir Woorman's study. "Where have you been, constable?" said the inspector.

"I took a tour of the apartment to make sure Raffles hasn't been anywhere," White countered. Then he took over from the inspector, who stretched out on the sofa and fell into a deep sleep after five minutes.

White pulled out his watch. "It's one o'clock," he muttered. "So I don't have but a few hours to say goodbye to Sir Woorman personally."

The time crept by slowly. Constable White had long since stopped looking at the room in which the safe was. He sat down at Sir Woorman's desk and was careful about the chair creaking. He straightened up and listened.

A sound repeated itself. He got up quietly and crept to the window through which he could peer into the room where the safe was.

Truly! There was a burglar in there! A skinny young fellow of about seventeen pushed open the door, which had been half-opened by a lockpick, and at the moment when Constable White turned his attention to him, he opened the safe.

The young man grabbed inside; but with a face of bitter disappointment he withdrew his hand again. The safe was empty. At that moment, Constable White cautiously opened the door and stepped inside the adjoining room.

The burglar uttered a suppressed scream, leaned against the wall in horror and looked at the constable with glazed eyes, while a tremor ran through his whole form.

"Well, you don't have that much courage right now, my boy," said White comfortably. "How did you get in here?"

"I've been hiding in the corridor since this afternoon," slurred the questioned young man. White eyed him more closely. He was a pitiful-looking person whose hollow cheeks clearly indicated need and misery.

"Why did you want to steal, boy?"

"Oh, that's worthless now. Take me with you and everything will have come to an end."

"Well, just wait a minute, sir! Just give me a reasonable answer. You never saw a safe before, have you?

"No, Mr. Constable, it's the very first time! I have never sneaked into someone else's property! You can tell. And why this time? Because, because, my mother dies if she can't be looked after better. The doctor said that. And I have no one but her. And she'll die, she'll die for sure!"

Constable White stood in front of the boy in silence for a while. "What's your name?"

"Harry Forester, Mr. Constable."

"Harry Forester? But where do you live, boy?"

"We live on Gerrard Street, Constable."

"So, so. Ah, that's strange after all." The constable reached into his pocket and drew a £100 note.

"Do you know what that is, Harry Forester? That's a hundred pounds. You can buy a lot of bread, wine, meat and medicines. Is that enough?"

The boy didn't know what to do. He looked now at the open safe, now at the constable, then he hit his forehead with his fist so loud it was audible, to make sure that he was not dreaming.

Constable White, however, put the hundred-pound note in his pocket, swept him into the dark room where Inspector Baxter was sleeping, and said: "Now you can go down the stairs. When a constable asks, you say you live in this house."

The youth nodded. He wanted to thank the policeman but he refused.

But just as the thief was about to leave the apartment, the door was ripped open and Sir Woorman entered.

Constable White quickly pushed the boy into a dark corner. Sir Woorman, however, hurried into his study and had scarcely seen a glimpse of a breached safe when he made such a noise that constables rushed in from all sides. The boy used this moment of confusion to hide.

"I am robbed!" shouted Sir Wooman, "Ten thousand pounds have been taken out of my safe. Ten thousand pounds! And you, inspector, you watched! Where's the thief? Where's the guy who stole my ten thousand pounds? Where's Raffles?"

Inspector Baxter stood next to Sir Woorman, completely bent. It had never happened to him before! That exceeded the limits of man if he had really not seen Raffles. There was only one thing left, that White saw everything after all.

But Constable White slowly took off his helmet and

likewise his wonderful wig, while all those standing by were petrified with shock and awe. Taking his time he removed the uniform overcoat and pulling out his revolver turned to Sir Woorman and said:

"I have the honor to introduce myself to you. I am Raffles." Then he turned to Baxter.

"I was convinced from the start that I would not be able to learn a lot in Scotland Yard, Inspector, but I still enjoyed a practical training. Thank you, boss, for teaching me all the Scotland Yard methods. You are all very nice! All respect!"

Then again Raffles turned to Woorman while the room was silent: "How can you lie so easily, Sir Woorman? Not a penny was in your safe! Raffles wasn't interested in breaking into it! But I kept my promise. If you want to inspect your other safe you will learn."

"Get him!" roared Sir Woorman. "Get him, constable."

With that he threw himself without pity on Raffles, who had already expected it. By half-kneeling on his right knee and pressing his left foot, he punched the onrushing Sir Woorman in the stomach with such force that he nearly did a somersault and collapsed with a groan.

In the next moment Raffles avoided the chain of constables, still coming. He slogged down the hall, threw open the door, and hurried to the stairs. An unfortunate coincidence, however, meant that a patrol of two constables, lured by the noise, stepped on to the stairs. Arriving on the top floor, Raffles swung himself from the window parapet in front of his horrified previous colleagues, grabbed a lightning rod on an adjacent building, let himself down two floors like an arrow, jumped into an open window and closed it behind him before the constables, who blindly pressed their heads through the skylight, could orient themselves in the dark and see where Raffles had gone.

Chapter II

Fatal Surprises

Lister took a closer look around the room he was in. Although he had forsaken the coat, he stood there fully dressed, for he had worn a casual dress suit under his uniform.

At first he saw nothing, for there was complete darkness. No sound could be heard. So he felt his way along the wall, carrying the electric light to aid in immediate emergency escape.

But nothing moved. He was in a luxuriously furnished bedroom. His gaze slid to the bed from which a silk atlas blanket had slipped down.

With astonishment he saw a young girl. It was evident that she was sleeping, as the light was off and she had not awakened. The sleeper was very attractive. The blonde hair flowed in broad strands over the lace-covered pillow. The left hand lay next to her chest, the right hung casually over the edge of the bed.

Raffles approached her quietly. Now when he looked around again, he saw a certain disorder in the room. An armchair by the mattress had overturned. A dresser had been thrown open, a picture knocked off the wall.

Raffles bounced back in horror when he looked sharply at the scene.

She was dead!

He put his hand carefully on the bedspread and pulled it back a little. Then he saw clearly dark, black-rimmed wide stripes that were sharply outlined on the young lady's neck. In a long breath he drew air through his nose.

"Aha!" he muttered. "First stunned, then strangled!" The initial light of dawn penetrated the window. Raffles took one more long, painful look at the unfortunate woman who had sustained such a mysterious death here. Then he opened the door and stepped out.

But again he bounced back in shock when his gaze fell into the corridor. There was a slight draft through the opening of the door. The maid's corpse, still wearing the white cap on her dark hair, swayed to and fro. She was hanging on a rope nailed to the wall.

"Terrible!" Raffles pushed out between his teeth. At first glance he hesitated seeing these awful things. But then the desire to find out more about the crime prevailed, perhaps to find the opportunity to give the wretched criminal his reward for his momentary indulgence.

So Raffles walked from room to room. The apartment consisted of seven chambers and was luxuriously appointed. Every piece of furniture, every picture testified both to the taste and to the wealth of the owner.

He, Raffles, found nothing in particular, nothing that could have given him any clue as to the identity of the murderer.

Only in the cloakroom there was a ribbon that was apparently worn around the arm or around the knee. It said:

"*Honny soit, qui mal y pense.*" (Shame on him who thinks bad of it.)

Underneath he could read the tiny words "Ribbon Men" (English Order of the Garter).

He took the band and put it in his pocket. Then he left the apartment silently. Outside the door hung a sign that read:

Madam de Vales.

Avoiding the gaze of the doormen the master thief left the house and went to Gerard Street. After a short search he located the house in which Mrs. Forester lived with her son. He wanted to see for himself whether the boy's statements were based on truth, and that he had become a burglar out of need, out of bitterest misery. But he was far more interested in the mysterious coincidence that seemed to exist between Sir Woorman and Mrs. Forester.

Lord Lister climbed the stairs and knocked on the little

door on which was a visiting card with the name: Alice Forester. When there was no answer, he opened it and went inside.

The first thing he saw was a still youthful woman of about thirty-five. She was lying in the middle of the floor, surrounded by a wide pool of blood. And still the red branch of life trickled from the terrible wound. A dagger with terrific force had cut her throat.

Raffles clenched his fists and staggered back to the door.

Even for his steely nerves, this confrontation of crimes, his unwanted witnessing of two in a short time was too much. But after the first shock he knelt down next to the unfortunate woman, in the hope of still being able to help her –but her life was already worthless.

Raffles himself took away several bloodstains after touching the dead body. He jumped up and looked around the small room. The boy's bed was in a tiny side hallway. In the room itself was Mrs. Forester's bed; an old worm-eaten dresser, a couple of chairs and a table, as well as a chest instead of a sofa, completed the poor furnishings.

The first thing Raffles got out was the question: "Why was this unlucky woman murdered? To whom was her bitterest poverty not enough? What had the unfortunate woman done to deserve such a fate?"

While Raffles was preoccupied with these thoughts and full of compassion and horror looked down at the dead woman, the door suddenly opened and the boy, whom he had surprised at the break-in the previous night, entered.

He glanced at the body. The blood formally fled from his cheeks. He went deathly pale—in the next moment he turned his eyes full of mad anger on the lord. He jumped over the table, grabbed a knife and wanted to atack the supposed murderer, but seeing the Great Unknown's raised revolver he shrunk back in horror.

"Put the weapon down, boy," said Lister, "and I'll put down mine. I'm Raffles, and Raffles isn't a murderer, you know." Only now did the boy recognize the savior of the previous night, although he could not figure anything out of what had happened, he was nevertheless convinced that this man could not possibly have been his mother's murderer. His legs buckled, but Lord Lister picked him up.

"Where did you go tonight?" was his first question.

"I was at home," replied the boy, who kept throwing himself sobbing over his mother's corpse, "and went out this morning to get some groceries.

"You have no idea who murdered your mother? You don't you have the slightest suspicion?"

"Not one, Mr. Raffles," replied the former.

Now Lister opened all the drawers. He searched the dead woman's correspondence, and while the boy crouched over the corpse, half-fainted from the cruel joke, without paying any attention to the actions of his secretive friend, the master thief read the letters of these unfortunates, which revealed the whole picture of the poor woman's life.

Suddenly he looked at him. "Do you know Sir Woorman, boy?"

"I worked in his office for a short time, Mr. Raffles," he replied to the question. "Otherwise I don't know anything about him."

It was a bitter smile that played on the master thief's lips as he left the house. He went to the closest public telephone and asked to speak with Mr. John Baxter, Police Inspector at Scotland Yard. The following conversation ensued:

"This is Baxter."

"This is Raffles"

"What?"

"This is Raffles?"

"That's not funny!"

"But I thought you were the funny one. The police always make bad jokes, my dear Baxter. But I'm not in the mood for spirits. There's a dead body at 17 Gerard Street. Mrs. Forester was murdered. You see, Inspector, it would be better if you got out of trouble with the London people by catching the mysterious murderers, instead of chasing after me all the time, a job that will piss you off forever."

"A corpse, you say? And did you discover it? What, are you on Gerard Street? Where are you now?"

"Now I'm on a pay telephone five minutes from Gerard

Street. By the time you come, my dear Baxter, I'll be somewhere else. Do not be under any illusions about it. Besides, you will have more to do today. There are two bodies at 29 Pall Mall Street, second floor on the left. Mistress and servant."

"You're kidding, Mr. Raffles! Three crimes in one night?"

"Is that a miracle, Inspector, when you spend the night in strange people's apartments? I already told you before that you're what they call in the Colonies 'All hat and no cattle.' If I were a police inspector, you couldn't be Raffles. But since I am convinced that you will not catch the criminal who murdered the unfortunate Mrs. Forester, I'm telling you that I will send the fellow to you within twenty-four hours. That's it."

Baxter turned away from the phone with a curse. "That Raffles!" he shouted, stretching his hands to heaven. "That Raffles! Raffles as a detective! It's laughable! He wants to cleanse London of murders! He wants to catch those who can get by me! Let the devil fetch him skin and hair!" After venting his anger in this way, he ordered three constables to drive with him. In a frenzied hunt they went to the telephone on Gerard Street.

"Have you seen Raffles?" said the inspector to the officer who was on patrol around the telephone.

"Raffles? Not a trace!"

"He was here a quarter of an hour ago!"

"Uh, you mean the elegant young man who used the phone? He's been gone a long time! But he's noble, and if it's

Raffles, he's doubly noble!"

The inspector hurried on and stomped into Mrs. Forester's apartment five minutes later with his officers. Drowned by grief, the boy looked up and measured the officers with a gloomy, hostile look.

"Here we have the guy who committed the murder!" shouted the inspector. "How did you get here? What are you doing here? Quickly—don't think about your answers first!"

"How did I get here?" replied the boy with a scornful smile. "Do you think that my mother's death does not matter to me?"

"Is the dead woman your mother?" said the inspector. "That doesn't change anything at all! Where have you been tonight?"

"Out! How can I defend myself when you've already passed judgement. Incidentally, since I was gone, I cannot be my mother's murderer!"

"Right! Right!" replied Baxter. "So prove your alibi! Then everything is all right! Where have been all night?"

"In the—" but then he paused. Should he state that he broke into Sir Woorman's? And that he had been able to slip away from him and the fact that the fake constable had let him?

He stayed silent. But that didn't bother Inspector Baxter much. He made the boy sit up and took him to the police station. The unfortunate lad was charged with suspicion of murdering his mother, made worse because of the hundred pound note they found on him.

Raffles was sitting in a cafe when he heard the news that the boy had been arrested. "I should have known it!" He muttered to himself, paid the check, called a cab and gave an address. "Dr. Smith, Lawyer, Regent Street." Ten minutes later the car stopped. Raffles climbed the carpeted stairs and rang the bell.

The lawyer was a man of about thirty-two. A scent of perfume was always his companion. Lord Lister took his cue and began: "You're the lawyer for Sir Woorman, Mr. Smith?"

"Well."

"Well, you are known to be an excellent lawyer. You have probably read that young Forester was arrested on charges of murdering his mother."

Mr. Smith appeared startled at the name's mention. "Well," he replied, taking pains to give his voice an evenly courageous sound. "Certainly."

"I should like you to take the poor guy's defense. That's all! You have to do everything to get him free immediately!"

The lawyer looked at his visitor with wide, malicious eyes. "And why, if I may ask?"

"Because he's innocent."

"Do you know that for sure?"

"Otherwise I would not come to you."

"Well, I got to know the guy because he worked temporarily in my office. I don't like him, so I won't defend him."

Raffles smiled. "You're a lawyer, aren't you? So don't you have the right to defend yourself in case of any trap? And just because you can't stand the poor boy that's no reason to not take over his defense."

"You can save yourself, sir, talking about platitudes. I defend the one who pays me."

"Ah so," said Raffles, pulling out a wallet. "How much do you require?"

Mr. Smith threw a long, covetous look at the wallet, but then turned pale again and replied: "I am not taking the defense."

"Then you have another reason. Perhaps one that is completely dishonorable. It seems to me, Mr. Smith, you are a rather suspicious person."

The lawyer had jumped up. In a flash his hand reached for the bell that connected the study to the office. But Raffles's left arm just as quickly caught it and threw his hand back.

"We don't need any witnesses," said the lord darkly. "Don't you find that you resemble me? That could easily put you in a position to be mistaken for Raffles."

"Raffles!" he screamed violently, staggering backwards. "You are Raffles. Help! Help!"

"Be quiet!" Lord Lister snapped at him; he had suddenly changed completely. He stood there tautly in front of the lawyer and piercingly fixed his eye so hard on the lawyer's gaze it was like he was looking inside his head. He formally fixed the attorney's eyes to himself, and suddenly the lawyer's raised right arm sank limply.

"Take your hat and your coat," ordered the master thief. The lawyer instinctively obeyed. The Great Unknown did not let him out of sight for a second. For the first time in a long while he awoke a phenomenal power that slumbered within him.

His iron will's force now paralyzed Mr. Smith's thoughts and brought him completely into the power of the man who stood over him like a statue...

Half an hour later a smartly dressed gentleman came to Scotland Yard and asked to speak to Inspector Baxter.

"Here I am," said the requested officer, who had heard the visitor's words. The stranger bowed very politely without looking at the Inspector. His behavior in general was very strange. He was already stumbling over the threshold and, in one word, behaving awkwardly.

"How can I help you, mister?" said Inspector Baxter at the suspicious man.

"My name is Mr. Smith," he answered. "I am an attorney and I live on Regent Street."

Inspector Baxter bowed.

"Now I remember seeing your picture in the papers, Mr. Smith. How can I serve you?"

The lawyer sat down.

"Where are you holding Harry Forester?"

"He's still with us here in Scotland Yard. He remains in police custody until the judge says otherwise."

"So, so! Is it possible to see the boy? I wish to interrogate him as I am convinced that he is innocent."

Inspector Baxter laughed.

"You want to take on his defense, Mr. Smith?"

"I do."

"Well, you're not very lucky."

"That's my business, Inspector. Produce the young man."

Harry Forester was brought five minutes later. The constable who led him in stood on his right. Mr. Smith kept a sharp eye on the door and exchanged a few irrelevant words with Harry Forester. He suddenly jumped up and yelled at the boy:

"Run, boy, as fast as your legs can carry you."

Harry, having little faith in London's justice, didn't have to be told twice. In no time he was around the corner. Baxter put his paw to his lips to summon the constables and ran to follow on the fugitive at the same time.

But Smith threw himself at him. A wild struggle arose between the two men, in which the inspector slipped and fell to the ground. A constable found it necessary to come to the rescue. In no time at all Mr. Smith was handcuffed. His collar was torn, his suit ripped to pieces. He stood shivering, pale in front of the officials, while his eyes suddenly took on a completely different expression and he looked around him, half horrified, half curious.

Now Baxter looked him up and down.

"But that's Raffles!" he cried, slapping his thigh. The constable agreed.

"The similarity was only noticeable, Inspector, when the guy stepped through the door."

"Raffles! Of course, how could I be so blind? This is Raffles!" shouted the inspector, performing a formal St. Vitus dance with pleasure.

The other stiffened his body. "You're crazy," he replied. "I am Smith."

"Ha, ha, excellent! This is the lawyer Mr. Smith."

"I demand that you set me free immediately if you do not want me to appear before the Supreme Court!" said the prisoner now seriously angry. "In the devil's name how did I get here? Was I drunk?"

Baxter raised an eyebrow. "Don't play the wild man. Your tricks don't work on me."

"But I tell you that I'm the lawyer Mr. Smith," the other yelled, cherry-red in the face.

"Well, we'll know soon enough," said Baxter comfortably, and went to the phone and looked up a number. "Office 17, No. 9763, Attorney Smith on the phone? Yeah? I have here a guy that I surely recognize as Raffles. He claims to be Mr. Smith. All right. Thank you very much, Mr. Smith."

Inspector Baxter turned and said to the prisoner. "Well,

Raffles, do you want to keep playing your hoax? Mr. Smith told me over the phone that he was in his office."

"But that's unbelievable," shouted the accused man, whom the constable was forcefully holding. "This is impossible! I can't sit in my office and be captured here.

"But—" suddenly there was a break in the prisoner's hitherto rigid and tormented procession. "Ah—now I remember what happened. Come on, Inspector, don't waste a second. The person who sits in my office is Raffles."

The inspector laughed so hard he doubled over. "You'd like to embarrass me again, Raffles, huh? Nothing will come of it this time, my friend! March, constable, take him; I will inform the judge about this very interesting catch."

The prisoner screamed, tugged, raged and roared, and fell into a fit that desperately resembled madness, but it did not help. He was taken to the police station and locked in a cell.

Meanwhile, the scene returns to Mr. Smith in his Regent Street office. But he wasn't Mr. Smith, he was Raffles, who had just comfortably lit a Henry Clay cigar. Outside, in the large office, which was separated from the study by an anteroom, there were around twenty employees. Raffles, in Mr. Smith's suit, smiled gleefully to himself.

How splendid it was! By gathering his energies and pressing his unusual will into the eyes of his counterpart, he sent Mr. Smith to Scotland Yard to free the harassed Harry Forester. He could do it without force. Lord Lister had told him how. He would knock down one constable, then open the door and let Forester run away.

The phone rang. It was Baxter and the lord said what he wanted him to say. Then he sat down at the desk, smiling again, opened it and searched the drawers. Then he, whom all the employees took to be Mr. Smith because of his resemblance—and he was still wearing the boss's suit—requested Sir Woorman's file, which he took with him into the attorney's private apartment adjoining the study to examine.

When he returned to his office, he carried a long robe, which he tucked under his arm.

The head clerk knocked on the door and entered. "Sir Woorman will speak to you, Mr. Smith."

Lister nodded, wrinkled his face seriously and said, "Bring him in."

Sir Woorman came in. Without looking at the lawyer he closed the door behind him and spread himself out in front of the desk.

"Mr. Smith, I thought you were my friend. At least it seemed like it for seven years. But you are not only not my friend anymore, but you are also defending a very miserable traitor, a bandit! You deserve to be kicked out of the band wearer's club."

Raffles did not pretend to be a little surprised. "What's the matter, Sir Woorman? What's wrong with you?"

The Irishman blushed with anger. "Are you still

pretending, Mr. Smith? I'll shoot you down on the spot, you crook! Didn't you promise to help me break this profitable matter with Mrs. Forester getting her kicked out in the world? And now that I see the goal, where her son would have been brought to trial for matricide and convicted, you come along and want to take on the boy's defense?"

"Who told you that?" said Raffles with a laugh.

"It's already in the papers," yelled Sir Woorman. Indeed, the real Mr. Smith, on the way to Scotland Yard, had informed a line-hungry journalist that he was going to defend Harry Forester.

"You will correct this situation at once," Sir Woorman ordered in a threatening tone.

"I don't think so," said Raffles without smiling.

"Have I not paid you ten thousand pounds for this so far, Mr. Smith?"

"I'll ask for another five thousand pounds in cash," Raffles put in.

Sir Woorman replied screaming, "Are you crazy! Do you want to take all my money from me? I'll pay you a thousand pounds if you ask for Harry Forester to be arrested and sentenced again. But not a penny more".

The pseudo-attorney shrugged. "I am very sorry, Sir Woorman. Five thousand pounds and not a penny less.

Sir Woorman haggled. But the false Smith was adamant. Finally Sir Woorman put five thousand pounds on the table.

"That's pretty much the last thing I own," he groaned.

"That will be another lie from you," said his counterpart. "I am sure you are still hiding double that somewhere. Five thousand and five thousand makes ten thousand. I think, Sir Woorman, it is worth it."

"What do you mean by that?" said Sir Wooman, getting angry and staring at the lawyer.

"Well, didn't I make your safe a thousand pounds lighter just last night, sir?"

At these words the person addressed drowned. Then his face went green and he screamed. "You're Raffles!"

"Well, yes, I'm Raffles!" Sir Woorman wanted to pounce on his enemy, but at the same moment the thief displayed a revolver. "Now to the point, I have several other things to say to you." With these words Lord Lister took all the steam out of his adversary. Pale with fear, Woorman sank back into a chair. Following every movement of the Master Thief, he suddenly jumped up, grabbed the revolver in a flash and held it on Raffles.

"Get down on your knees, coward, you're my prisoner."

Raffles laughed. "It's not loaded at all, Sir Woorman, why go to so much trouble?"

At that moment there was a loud noise on the stairs, and immediately afterwards Inspector Baxter rushed up with a couple of constables. In their midst was Mr. Smith.

John Raffles half-twisted himself to keep an eye on the people streaming in through the jerked door, as did Sir

Woorman, who had bent down in amazement at the revolver and examined the weapon to see whether it was actually empty.

"Here's the scoundrel!" shouted Baxter. "Forward! At him, boys! The Raffles convention has come to an end."

Mr. Smith, the lawyer whose real identity had been clarified in the court, screamed, spitting: "Lord, you–how could you have allowed yourself to do such a trick? Are you a living devil?"

In the first moment of the hustle and bustle, when Raffles seemed to have been denied every chance of escape, four floors up in an elegant house, the Great Unknown had jumped from his desk into the corner of the room with a single leap, so that he was in a moment it was between it and the man who brought the constables.

The next instant they saw something in Raffles's hand that at first glance nobody could recognize. "Back off," shouted the Great Unknown, "not a step further. The first one who tries to arrest me dies."

The constables hesitated.

"Be sensible, Raffles," said Baxter uneasily. "There's no point in that. You are in my power so now the smartest thing you can do is surrender."

Lord Lister's face had changed terribly. His eyes had become unnaturally wide, his lips were pressed together threateningly. "Not one step, I say," he called again, while he laughed inwardly, assuming the pose of a desperate man who, cornered, will no longer shrink from anything.

"One more step, Inspector, and we'll all be blown up together."

He stood there, threatening, arms raised. Nobody dared answer while all eyes were on Lord Lister's hands. But John Raffles said to the lawyer:

"You should thank me, Mr. Smith, and since I believe that a scoundrel like you—for a lawyer who makes himself a criminal middleman is a scoundrel—does not want to owe a favor to a villain like me, I urge you to pay me £3,000—you probably have that much in your private apartment."

Mr. Smith was rigid. In this situation, now that Raffles was singing, he liked to play the winner with incredible calm and to demand as much money from him as the lawyer had in a small safe in his apartment.

'You're crazy," he shouted, foam creeping from his lips. "We're negotiating with an animal!"

"I sure hope so," replied Raffles. "And don't be under any illusions about the weapon!"

"Come on, Inspector Baxter, are you going to keep hesitating until this guy—"

But he couldn't speak, because Raffles had already raised his arm again—just a moment, and everyone was shattered, torn to pieces. What kind of terrible weapon did he hold between his thumb and forefinger?

"Stop—stop!" shouted Mr. Smith, whose life was worth

three thousand pounds. "I'll get him the money." With trembling knees, Mr. Smith walked away while Raffles, laughing, changed his position so that he could completely overlook the room in which Mr. Smith's small safe was. Simultaneously with his left hand he grabbed the revolver that Sir Woorman had put down on the desk, while his right hand was still threateningly holding the mysterious thing in the air.

"Mr. Smith!"

"What?"

"Don't get lost! I'm watching! Stick to the plan! You'll have to spend a lot of money if you don't want me to shoot through your ribs one after the other! I'm a great shot, Mr. Smith, and this revolver has six chambers."

Trembling, Mr. Smith obeyed, while Baxter and his constables faced the fearsome man in doubt, unable to come to an independent thought. Mr. Smith believed that three thousand pounds was a harsh penalty, but it could be worse: Raffles would take the ten thousand sitting in a fireproof box outside in the office where his people worked. Now he cursed the hour when he had a soundproof wall built into the adjoining room separating his chamber from the employees' office so that they could never overhear his client negotiations.

This made it possible for such a fateful scene to take place here without his people hearing the slightest bit. Inspector Baxter made one more desperate attempt, but Raffles scared him back. At that moment Mr. Smith entered with the money. Raffles told him to put it on the desk and back away. The lawyer obeyed, trembling. Raffles stepped away from the desk, took the money, flew to the exit that led into the anteroom, and suddenly ripped open the door intending to disappear. At that moment, Baxter, who had thought what boundless embarrassment he would reap this time if he let Raffles slip away, threw himself against the half-open door with deathly contempt.

He was already stretching out both arms towards Raffles—who at that moment, snatched up a lighter from the desktop, and moved a burning flame close to the mysterious object that he still had in his hand. It would have been easy for Baxter to knock the creepy thing out of it, but when the Police Inspector saw the lighter flare, he was sure the whole house would be blown up in an instant. He staggered back—but at the same time something happened that no one had expected, and it produced a horrific, terrible effect:

The master thief suddenly was shrouded in smoke and haze. He disappeared. From the place where he stood, however, a glowing spray closed on Baxter and his constables. Hissing, wheezing, crackling and puffing, it flew in a wide fiery arc, burning and landing right into the middle of the police officers, so that they howled and screamed in horror. In the confusion they could not find a door, as the whole room was suffused with smoke through which the glowing sparks spurted. The chamber seemed ready to go up in flames, as if all the good constables were suddenly to lose their lives in a terrible explosion.

Baxter fell to the ground in horror. Mr. Smith, uttering the last cry of death, threw himself out onto the ground and stretched on all fours, convinced that he must find death in the flames that drowned the whole room.

Suddenly the spray stopped. At first one saw nothing but smoke, mist and steam. Then Baxter rose from the floor, half afraid and blinded, half angry, and said:

"I think it really stinks badly in here."

The fact, which the brave police inspector had spoken aloud, brought his constables halfway back to their consciousness. They crawled over and rose slowly from the ground, pale as death, with trembling knees. And Baxter with big eyes looked over the room, gritted his teeth, hit his forehead three times with his fist as if imploringly and screamed: "Heaven and Hell! The whole thing came from fireworks. Oh, Raffles, you are a plague!"

The constables rushed, ashamed, to the place where Raffles had stood, but he was gone. The officers remained there in silence, with their necks bent forward. No one would dare look at the other in shame, because the fact that they had said their last prayer when a rocket began to burst out was surely a unique example in the annals of London police history. The only sound that could be heard at first was that which came from the key with which Raffles locked the door of the study in the anteroom. Now Mr. Smith crawled up, blue in the face with anger, and yelled:

"Is that possible, Inspector Baxter? Did you let a rocket scare you half to death? A rocket? Don't you know what fireworks are? And you and your clumsy constables run away from phony smoke. Not a shame, Inspector? A rocket! If the London criminals hear that, that won't make us any safer, Inspector. Do you belong to a monastery or Scotland Yard?"

"Refrain from such insolence, Mr. Smith," Baxter cried in rage. "Why did I get so confused? By your terrified behavior, Mr. Smith! If you hadn't howled like a fox terrier kicked out from his hind paws, I could have kept calm and cold blooded!"

"Me? Did I cry? Inspector, I forbid—".

So it went on. Not much was missing from the fight, as the two heroes almost came to blows. Precious time was now forgotten, and when Baxter finally remembered Raffles was missing it was too late.

Raffles didn't tarry. After locking the door behind him, he had picked up a second coat, as well as Mr. Smith's top hat, two pieces of clothing that had been hanging in the anteroom, slipped on the coat, put on the hat and turned up his collar so that you could only see the tip of his nose properly. Then he went to the office where Mr. Smith's staff worked.

"Mr. Brown!" he said to the first clerk, imitating Mr. Smith's voice with perfect calm.

"Mr. Smith?"

"Open the cash register for me." The accountant took from his waistband the custodial keys and opened the safe.

Raffles saw ten thousand pounds in front of him. He hesitated for a moment.

"If I'm not mistaken, we have the first tomorrow, huh?"

"Right, Mr. Smith!"

"How much did you need to pay the salaries?"

"A hundred and fifty pounds, Mr. Smith."

"That's right! Well, I think you have all done your duty in an incredibly special way lately! As a bonus, I'll pay you six-month's salary. Are you satisfied with that?"

"Oh!" the first clerk marveled when he looked at his colleagues with a face that definitely questioned his boss' sanity.

Raffles put a £1,000 note on the table. pocketed the nine thousand, lit his cigarette, and left the office while the accountant and the other clerks cheered him on. Downstairs he got into a cab and continued.

When Mr. Smith returned to the office with the inspector and the constables after the fruitless hunt, he was clear.

All the employees had preferred to retire for a few weeks, given the incredible generosity of their boss, all the more as if they weren't quite sure that the money would suddenly disappear in their boss's absence.

Baxter stood before the empty safe, eyes wide. He pulled out his hair, hit his forehead over and over with his fist and screamed: "It's madness! Pure madness! This Raffles is the first nail in my coffin! I will not live long!"

Mr. Smith turned with a grim face and said: "Well, after

your performance today, you really let yourself be buried,
Inspector."

Chapter III

The Ribbon Men

Lord Lister sat comfortably in a large armchair in his Victoria Street apartment. Charlie Brand, his friend and secretary, leaned against the fireplace.

"Well," Raffles continuing a previous conversation said, "have you found out what kind of club the Ribbon Men are? They seems unrelated to that secret society that was founded in Ireland in 1817 to protect the armed tenants against the attacks and violence of the rich landlords. Today these band members are hardly allowed to have the influence they had back then, when they gained such power that no one dared to appear in court against their attacks."

"You are absolutely right that you associated these modern Ribbon Men with historical Band Men," replied Charlie Brand. "I also immediately thought of what you just touched on, and the fact that the ribbon contains the message: *Honny Soit, qui mal y pense*, which you showed me, displayed with gold writing on a blue background. That reminded me of another historic group of ribbon wearers, since the Band Court, another name for that ribbon society, also wore blue bands.

"So I surreptitiously studied all of London's noble circles and am in the excellent position to be able to give you an exhaustive explanation."

"Ah, I can't wait!" said Lord Lister.

"The Ribbon Men are a secret society—and a lodge like the shadowy Freemasons, because upscale London knows about their existence as well as the police. But the young people, who incidentally are said to have had several dark stories kept out of the woods, are tolerated because they belong to the highest circles of the city's population."

Lord Lister nodded.

"I already knew that the police didn't think it necessary to have a better look at the rulers. And where is the headquarters of this modern kangaroo court?"

"At No. 39 St. James Street.

Lord Lister's ears picked up. "Ah! So there! Well, the

rulers have already made quite unpleasant acquaintance with my fists."

"How so? Have you met them yet?"

"Yes. At the time when I was doing half a year of apprenticeship as Constable White at Scotland Yard. Well, I'm not at all surprised that this famous Sir Woorman is a member of the Ribbon Men. Heard the good lawyer Smith is, too, as the robe I found on him proves, and which should give me the opportunity to study the mysterious arrangements of this lodge more closely."

With these words Lord Lister spread the blood-red robe with a similar hood in front of Charlie Brand. It was cut exactly like that of the old German feudal judges and had only two holes in the hood for the eyes. A blue ribbon shimmered on the wide, fluffy silk sleeve, and it read: *Honny soit, qui mal y pense.*

"I took this from Mr. Smith," Lister laughed.

"But how do you know that Sir Woorman is also a member of this society?" said his secretary.

"I already told you, dear Charlie, that I had a reunion with some of these guys on St. James Street when they chased a young girl. It was too dark for me to make her out, and the matter happened very quickly.

"But I recognized Sir Woorman by his voice the first moment I heard him speak, because he had been the main screamer among the gang."

Charlie Brand looked at the floor pensively for a while.

"You told me that you found the blue band with the saying in the murdered Madam de Vales's apartment, didn't you?"

Lord Lister laughed. "I know what you want to say, my boy. This ribbon will lead to the discovery of the perpetrator. I'll see whose robe is missing theirs tonight when I visit the Ribbon Men. Besides, I can already guess who it is. Despite searching, I could not discover a penny of her fortune. But it is suspected that she was extraordinarily rich, according to Sir Woorman."

Charlie Brand rocked his head doubtfully. "Villain! Don't you think he was Mrs. Forester's killer too?"

"That's right, dear Charlie. To come back from the previous matter, I should like to point out that some of the banknotes I found at Sir Woorman's and some of those that Mr. Smith gave me voluntarily consisted of French West African francs. As for Mrs. Forester, it is stated that Sir Woorman had relations with her eighteen years ago. At that time he was still a poor fellow and no one would suspect that the former attorney would become so wealthy and influential.

"There are threatening letters from Mrs. Forester, who, evidently driven by her desperation and plight, informed her former lover that she would not spare him any further and that his earlier atrocities would be made public if he didn't finally decide to do something for his son at least. So poor Harry is Sir Woorman's son, who since he had his affair with Mrs. Forester seems to have been up to something. That too will probably be made clear. I heard that Mrs. Forester's husband died a sudden, unexplained death eighteen years ago. The young widow may

not have been entirely innocent of it. She received her sentence

after seventeen years. But the main culprit, Sir Woorman, is still

free and can dare to dupe the company. Fearing that Mrs.

Forester might really compromise him in her desperation, he

resolutely killed her and calmly let it happen that his boy was

sent to prison for twenty years on suspicion of killing his

mother.”

“And what about Mr. Smith, the criminal?”

“He knew everything, dear Charlie, and was silent. Yes,

he supported the machinations of his little client as much as

possible. Sir Woorman was very liberal with the money he stole

from the murdered Madame de Vales. You see, dear Charlie, this

time I have come into the company of quite honorable people!

“Inspector Baxter’s gold watch holds the promise that

within twenty-four hours I would deliver Mrs. Forester’s

murderer to him. He shouldn’t say that I broke my word. You

know, dear Charlie, what you have to do. Don’t forget the

instructions, as much depends on it.”

“All right!” laughed Charlie. “You can rely on me.”

Lord Lister went down the stairs, got into his coupé, and

drove to St. James Street. The Band Men had their club on the

third floor of the building, which, incidentally, was still occupied

by two others one floor higher. Precisely at half past ten the

members gathered in a large hall, in which about six servants

with black masks passed around drinks and awaited the orders of their masters. None of the members could now recognize the other, for each was wearing his red costume, which covered the whole body and face and only exposed two twinkling eyes.

After the members of the club had gathered, one of them said, taking down one of the swords with which the walls were adorned:

"My brothers! We have again gathered for an extraordinary judgment, after I take the oath of allegiance from you, as is the law under the Ribbon Men."

The speaker began again: "Each member of the Ribbon Men swears with the most sacred oaths, by God, the devil and all their kin, to keep the laws of our club sacred, to submit to all judgements and verdicts of the Band Men and to do nothing against them or cause them harm. The Ribbon Men swear to help keep the club secret and to hide it from women and children, from father and mother, from sister and brother, from joy and wind, above everything on which the sun shines and the rain wets, and above all from everything between heaven and earth."

In the chorus everyone repeated this oath. When they had finished the speaker continued.

"Hear and know the laws of the Ribbon Men. Whoever does not keep the Holy Band Court, who betrays it, who starts anything that can harm it, should be corrupted by fire, water or poisons and all other gang men are stopped and obliged to kill him wherever they can get him, by water, by fire or by the sword."

The others repeated the oath again. After the laughable and dangerous ceremony was ended in this way, the Band Men took their seats. The chairs were set up in a large semicircle. On a raised podium was a table at which sat a mysterious figure that had an animal head and human body: the judge, evidently the recognized leader of this mysterious union.

The others were grouped around them. In the middle of the semicircle, however, stood a crude, ordinary wooden bench, the back of which was still green. It looked strange in this room, the walls of which were partly covered with ancient swords, pikes and rifles.

"Bring in accused to appear before court!" the bailiff ordered.

A door in the background was thrown open, and a young girl of extraordinary beauty was dragged in between the servants. Her rich blond hair flowed over the dark dress, which raw hands had partly torn. She looked around with crazy eyes that gleamed gloomily from her pale face, then the bailiff told her to take a seat on the bench in front of the judge.

She obeyed mechanically. Without a doubt she was convinced that she was caught in a dark dream, an illusion that was understandable, for no reasonable man could have conceived such a shameful comedy in the middle of London.

"Is your name Ellen Crofton?" began the judge. She looked at him with frowning eyes in which all her astonishment and horror were reflected at the same time. At the sound of that voice, she seemed to come to.

She jumped up, and both arms outstretched, she cried, while a shudder shook her body: "For all the world to hear, mercy! Have mercy on a girl who will go insane if you play your cruel game with her any longer!"

But she could just as well have looked at the terrible figure with the animal head and human body behind the judge's desk. She seemed to be in a crisis of confusion, caused by the dead or mysterious beings. She could read no expression, no judging eye, and she heard nothing but the voice of the judge, who began again.

"You should be served justice, lady, as the Band Court decides. Hear what we're accusing you of."

At that moment the porters who were closing off the hall were pushed back and a Band Man entered. The blue ribbon gleamed on his left arm. The red robe hid his figure, and calmly, as if he had long been known in this room, he stepped among the members to look for his place.

A whisper, a murmur, ran through the rows of Ribbon Men. For a moment it was like the silence of death over the room. There were twelve seats in the hall, but the one that had just entered was the thirteenth.

That was unheard of. The Band Men's eyes wandered around and quickly ticked off those present. It was twelve, the correct number. Who was he? A traitor? Or was he already among them? Was the one who just walked in a member and had someone previously sneaked in? Since none of the members recognized anyone else under the completely identical red robes, the horror at the appearance of the thirteenth was doubled.

The judge was silent for a while. Apparently he was wondering what to do at this fatal moment. Because with the appearance of the thirteenth calamity had been brought into the hall, that was certain. There was no doubt that there was a traitor among them. It was now a matter of managing the matter with skill in such a way that the twelve could finish the thirteenth without arousal of any kind. The judge therefore responded with a short nod to the thirteenth's greeting, who, without making the slightest change, leaned against the wall, crossed his arms and let his large, flashing eyes rest on Miss Crofton.

"Hear what the prosecution is bringing against you, lady," the judge went on, but without his voice sounding as assured as previously. "The Band Court accuses you of not upholding the honor of English women and girls. You are charged with being in a relationship with a man whose adventures are scandalous in London."

The poor, tormented girl looked around again with the crazy look as before. "I don't understand you," she said finally, flatly. "Whom are you talking about?"

"Sir Woorman!" replied the judge, while his eyes flashed scornfully.

Ellen Crofton screamed out. "Sir Woorman? I am supposed to have a relationship with Sir Woorman? My God, gentlemen, can I help if Sir Woorman torments me for weeks about becoming his wife? And you accuse me of - oh, how terrible! I hate him! I despise him! And if the honor of English ladies were everywhere as safe as it is with me, gentlemen, England sleeps peacefully!"

"Those are words, nothing but words," replied the judge, while his voice took on a sound from which one could clearly hear the shame of the already-fixed plan.

"The Band Court thinks you have been lost for a long time, lady," continued the judge. "You have recently shamefully tried to corrupt only honorable men who met in a club on St. James Street. The court's judgment is that you, Miss Crofton, should be flogged at this point, and each of the Band Men will be entitled to give you three blows."

A hamish triumph shone in the judge's eyes as he said these words. There was a slight movement among the assembled. The young girl, however, who apparently could not believe that such evil as the judge just demonstrated could exist, straightened up proudly and exclaimed:

"I want to see, gentlemen, which of you dares to attack an English lady!"

But when she saw that the masked servants, whose scornful smiles she could very well see because the masks did not cover their lips, when she saw shackles that were ready to bind her, when she could no longer doubt that she was in the power of wretched, common criminals, she threw herself on her knees. And while she was wringing her hands against everyone in the room, she cried: "For God's sake have mercy! I'm not afraid of any pain—but I haven't done anything to anyone that they have right to insult me! You would not do this terrible disgrace to an English lady! Mercy!"

But the immobile, blood-red masks revealed nothing of the feelings of those who hid themselves during this ruckus. The servants seized her with raw hands. Her cries for help were lost in the sounds of porters locking heavy doors.

At that moment one of the Band-Men stepped beside Miss Crofton. He made a few arm movements left and right and two masked servants flew against the wall and cracked their skulls.

Now the villains, who did not hesitate to commit low crimes under the protection of an apparently noble club, came to life. They wanted to throw themselves at the thirteenth man, because it was he who had suddenly stepped forward to save the young lady, but the leader's loud order held them back.

"Don't be in a hurry, my brothers!" he called out in a strong voice. "One of the Band Men seems to think it necessary to stand up for the defendant. Well, let him say what he can do in her defense."

Immediately they went quiet. Miss Crofton had pleadingly wrapped her arms around the knees of the man whose face neither she nor any of the others could see.

"This young lady," said a dull voice now, "is above

suspicion. Above all, rowdies like you must not dare to raise your hand against such innocent people. I do not recognize the judge's authority because he has forgotten to put on the blue ribbon that entitles him to feel like a member of the Band Men."

All eyes were on the judge. Indeed—he was the only one who didn't have the blue ribbon on his left sleeve. Now the suspicion was directed against the judge himself. For a few seconds an investigative atmosphere permeated the hall; then the thirteenth continued in a loud, raised voice:

"Here is the blue ribbon, Judge, that you lack!" While the Band Men's attention was aimed at the top, the thirteenth man presented the armband with the blue fabric, which they all saw, and the judge fastened it with trembling hands to his left sleeve. And his eyes stared with an eerie glow at the man who had handed him the ribbon - but he was silent. Then one of the Band Men stepped forward and said to the thirteenth:

"Release the girl who has been left to our control and say your name and who you are!"

At that moment, one of the other twelve Band Men went to the shoulder of the thirteenth and whispered to him:

"You are Raffles!"

The one to whom these words were addressed turned around, looked the masked man in the eye and replied:

"You are Inspector Baxter."

"OK. You are under arrest, Raffles."

"Not a bit of it! Take care, Baxter, and don't speak so

loudly, for you may not find anyone here cares for you. A police inspector among the Ribbon Men—Mr. Baxter, you may not be too happy with the results."

Baxter seemed to see that. Mr. Smith had understood that the red robe had been stolen from him. And the lawyer, realizing that Raffles was out to ruin him and Sir Woorman, had thought it best to give up the Band Men to save himself. That was why he had given the appropriate information to Baxter, who, convinced that Raffles in Mr. Smith's red robe would visit the club, had gone to arrest him there. Raffles would be thirteenth at the club even though Mr. Smith was absent.

Baxter pulled back a little. He was well aware that they would be far more likely to let Raffles get away than to put up with a police inspector, especially after he'd just witnessed the strange acts of the Ribbon Men. So he decided to wait for the appropriate moment to arrest Raffles.

In the meantime, the rest of the Ribbon Men began arguing against him. They wanted to snatch the girl from him. Suddenly someone shouted:

"We will decide this with weapons! I contend that this miserable man who dares to act contrary to the laws of the Band Court is a traitor, and traitors cannot leave the club alive!"

Suddenly the Band-Men's daggers flashed around Raffles. Ellen Crofton uttered a piercing scream, for she thought she would see the man who was so bravely protecting her fall in the next instant. But the thief held out a revolver against those struggling against him.

"Get back if you want to live!" he called out in a thunderous voice. But now the strangest thing happened that evening, something that none of the band members understood. Now it became clear that there was not one, but two traitors among them, because suddenly one of the masked men stood on the side of the attacked man and called out, also displaying a revolver that was ready to fire.

"Back! He is under my protection!"

It was Baxter who, fearing the Band Men might steal Raffles from him by killing him, put himself on the side of the man who persecuted him for so long. And it was more important for him when he finally remembered his authority to not allow the comedic role he was playing go so far as to allow a person to be murdered. Lister laughed under his robe for Baxter to hear.

"It's nice of you, Inspector," he said, "that you've suddenly become my friend."

"Just for five minutes, Raffles," Baxter replied grimly, while the Band Men had withdrawn in the immense confusion.

And their call grew louder and louder: "To arms! Get the weapons! Down with the traitors!"

Inspector Baxter suddenly felt fear creep into his heart when he saw the Band Men tearing their rapiers and swords from the walls. They did not dare shoot so as not to arouse the attention of one of the clubs above or below them, for the bang of the revolver would probably have penetrated outside.

While Baxter hesitated indecisively, Lord Lister with tremendous force had suddenly broken through to the wall that surrounded him, tore a sabre from the it, and immediately took up position next to the young lady.

"Come on, cowards!" he cried, the courage to fight threatened in his voice. "I want to show you how John Raffles knows how to fence!"

No sooner had the word Raffles reached the ears of the band members than it hung in the air like a paralyzing horror. Only a few of the bravest stepped towards the master thief with their sabers lifted. Baxter tried fervently to drive them back with his revolver. Since he dared not shoot at these men, because he feared the consequences that might arise from his nightly adventure, the attackers could not be further intimidated. Baxter was run over, and in the next instant half a dozen blades flashed around Raffles, who was pressing against him to protect them from the enemies. In the next moment, the blades flashed and clanked against each other. The band members now had to realize, however, that the guy who called himself Raffles knew how to deal with the blade much better than they did. His weapon whistled through the air, punched this way and that, parried the angry blows against his head, incapacitated two, knocked a third down and would had driven all the Band Men to the devil if the doormen hadn't suddenly burst in.

A tall constable emerged from behind the intrepid servants, who uttered their warning calls too late.

"In the name of the law—"

It looked like a bomb had gone off. In no time at all, the band members dashed apart in all directions. Baxter had lost sight of Raffles at the moment of general confusion when the Band Men had scattered like billiard balls.

The latter had released Miss Crofton, whom everyone forgot, and jumped like a tiger towards a door that was in the background of the room. It was through this door that the judge had fled, running away the moment the thirteenth had mentioned the mysterious name "Raffles." This ended up in a small side room. In the background there was a large iron safe, to the right of which there was a huge picture of Leda and the swan.

Raffles looked around for a moment. He had torn the hood off his head to breathe better. "I bet the gang keeps their secret files hidden in here," he muttered. "Who knows how these scriptures will pay off." In no time he had inserted a lockpick into the not-too-tight safe—the door flew open and in a feverish hurry Raffles extracted paper and hid them in his pocket. Then one of the Band-Men gasped breathlessly behind the Great Unknown.

Now that he had reached him, he too tore the hood off his head. He was Baxter.

"Finally! Thank God! You are under arrest, Raffles."

He was just putting the last of the papers in his pocket. "Inspector, I will never get tired of your affection," he said, turning his smiling face on him. "Didn't I promise to deliver

Mrs. Forester's murderer to you? You must absolutely allow me to keep my promise."

"The devil may allow you to do that," Baxter shouted, reaching out his hand to Lord Lister. "One more time, in the name of the law—". Suddenly the Great Unknown had grabbed the inspector's robe, pushed the end of it into the safe and slammed the metal door.

"That's just mean!" shouted Baxter, who slipped and fell on his nose trying to follow Raffles.

But Raffles had already disappeared. He slogged down the dark corridor. His keen, all-encompassing look had immediately recognized that the large painting which was set into the wall contained a secret door. Indeed, the instant he pressed a button on the picture it rotated in its frame and Raffles disappeared inside the wall.

At last Inspector Baxter managed to break free. He was desperately running up and down the corridor looking for Raffles when suddenly the constable came running in.

"Inspector!" he called.

"What the hell, what's up? Will you help me find Raffles?"

"I want that!" he said. "Come quickly. He fell out on the street! The whole band are already on the hunt for him."

Like a madman, Baxter rushed after the constable, who was whisking him and the club members, who had doffed their robes, down the stairs.

In the meantime Raffles found himself in a dark room. There was no exit here, he saw in the glow of the electric flashlight that he held. It was just a hiding place that the Band Men had created so that they could hide if necessary. But only one had visited it: the judge.

The other, in the initial confusion, was looking in all directions. Lister held up the electric lamp, the glow of which illuminated the judge's face. He had pulled the hood down and Raffle's big eyes were looking into Sir Woorman's features. Half-crouched, panting like a tiger, the muscular Sir Woorman was furious.

"Pig!" he hissed at him.

Raffles smiled. "You are wrong about the me, Sir Woorman. Or do you still think it necessary to be angry with me?"

"Miserable bandit! Dog!" roared the judge, for whom there was no longer any way out than to face his mortal enemy. "One of us has to die!" gasped Sir Woorman. "But the one will be Raffles, you, my wicked shadow, who dared to tie up with me!"

The lord smiled again. "Why should one of us die, Sir Woorman? Who will be so bloodthirsty? The world is big enough for the both of us!"

Sir Woorman took a deep breath. "Then—then, make way, Raffles, and let me through!"

Lord Lister turned the lamp tight so that it could no

longer go out, set it on the floor next to him, without taking his eyes off his enemy for a second, replied: "I don't think so, Sir Woorman."

"What are you going to do, Mr. Raffles?"

"I'll turn you over to the police because villains like you need to be dealt with."

Sir Woorman screamed like a beast. There was foam on his lips, his eyes rolled like wheels.

"Then die!" he hissed and threw himself on the lord, while his monkey-like long arm holding a sharp-edged dagger sliced through the air. But Raffles ducked skillfully, dodged the blade, slipped under Sir Woorman and grabbed his right arm so tightly that he involuntarily lowered the weapon.

Now, in the narrow hiding place, where the two men could bang their heads against the wall at any moment, a life-and-death wrestling match took place. Raffles himself had crushed the electric lamp when he stepped back. The light was out, and an impenetrable darkness fell over this terrible fight, which seemed to last forever, but in truth was decided in less than two minutes. Raffles had managed to free himself from the iron grip of his opponent for a moment. As Woorman was just pulling out the revolver to shoot Raffles down Lister used this opportune opening to suddenly slide his right knee behind Sir Woorman and hit him in the throat with his flaring hand. This jiu-jitsu blow pushed Sir Woorman backwards and he fell over his opponent's right knee.

The shot went into the ceiling. In no time Raffles was on the fallen man and pressed his knee on the chest of the breathless, wretched knight.

Sir Woorman pleaded in vain for mercy. "I'll pay you what whatever you want," he groaned.

Raffles laughed. "I'll take what I need myself, ass," he replied. In no time at all he had tied Sir Woorman with the ropes both men had worn around their robes so that he could no longer move. Then Raffles carefully and slowly opened the secret door. He looked around. He saw no one.

Then he opened the door that led into the Band Men's hall; it was empty. Raffles went back, tossed his opponent like a sack over his left shoulder and hauled him into the room and lay him down in the middle. Then he took a business card out of his pocket and wrote on it with a pencil:

"Dear Inspector Baxter! Exactly as I promised you, I am hereby delivering the murderer of Mrs. Forester, Madam de Vales and her maid.

"John C. Raffles."

The master thief took off the robe that was hanging from his body, straightened his informal suit, went into the anteroom, took his hat and stick and hung his cloak around his shoulders. At that moment the constable appeared before him, who by his appearance had dispersed the band members. "You can't go down there," he said. "The whole company is still racing around in the street looking for you. Baxter is downstairs with half a dozen constables and they're watching all the exits. Did I do my job well, Raffles?"

He put his hand on his shoulder. "Excellent, dear Charlie. It turned out exactly as I suspected."

"And I," his friend replied, "sent Inspector Baxter away in exactly the opposite direction from you. But now good advice is dear. You sit like the fox in a burrow; it is impossible for you to leave the house without being arrested."

Raffles thought for a moment. Then a mocking smile crossed his features. "Go back down, dear Charlie," he said, "and help Baxter guard the house. The moment you see me step out, you will divert his attention away from me with some meaningless speech."

The master thief's friend hesitated.

"It won't go well," he replied. "The rest of the constables would recognize any trick if you went out now."

"Who said anything about now?" replied Raffles with a smile. "I won't go before dawn. But if I leave the house with the members of the fashionable club on the second floor, no one will look for Raffles among them." With these words Lister fastened the band on which the words were written: *Honny soit, qui mal y pense*, around his knee and said, laughing, pointing at it: "Now I am a member of the Order of the Court and am Lord of Westminster, dear Charlie. Fine, what?"

And calmly he stepped down the stairs and wandered into the brightly lit anteroom of the Jockey Club, while the lackeys bowed to the ground before him. But the constable, shuddering with laughter, went down the stairs.

Baxter had taken off his red robes and was walking towards Charlie Brand, his face flushed. "Did you see him?"

"No, inspector. He made himself scarce."

"I have an idea!" Baxter said suddenly. "What could be more natural than that Raffles immerse himself in one of the ubiquitous clubs that are in the house? I'll go to the Jockey Club first."

The Inspector hurried up the stairs in long strides.

Charlie let his chin drop to his chest and mumbled: "My goodness! Now things go wrong."

Chapter IV

A Visit to the Lord Chancellor of the Treasury
of the United Three Kingdoms

"Lord of Westminster," loudly called the servant in the hall and bowed deeply to John Raffles, who, adorned with the Order of the Garter, entered the great club hall, where most of the gentlemen were seated at games. A few looked up, but most of them didn't care about the new guest. The gentlemen of the Jockey Club were the most distinguished members of the London aristocracy, so the Lord of Westminster did not appear an exceptional figure in these rooms.

Lord Lister must have known what he was doing when he chose that name. He had a fleeting resemblance to him and the game which the master thief dared was extremely dangerous, for he only needed to meet a close acquaintance of the lord to be lost. Therefore, without first waiting for the guests' attention to concentrate on him, he stepped to one of the gaming tables and sat down at it. At the small, improvised roulette station, the winning gentlemen were between twenty and forty years of age. The game was just interrupted when the Lord of Westminster took one of the empty chairs.

"I tell you, Marquis," cried the Earl of Westbury, "it is impossible to even peek into the vault where the King's medals are kept. They represent a value of untold millions."

The Marquis, an elegant Frenchman, stroked his mustache with his well-groomed hand. "Well, a man who combines courage with skill, surely it must be possible to get at them."

"You don't know the security of our police force and the vaults of the Lord Chancellor of the Exchequer in Buckingham Palace," replied the Earl.

Another, Lord Rathsborne, interjected: "Even Raffles, the Master Thief, would not be able to see the insignias, let alone attempt to steal one."

"Raffles!?" the Lord of Westminster now joined the conversation. "Who is Raffles? I have just come back from a trip and heard this name for the first time. New nobility, what?"

The gentlemen laughed.

"Well, lord, this is a new nobility! Don't know who Raffles is? Lord, you don't know London anymore! Raffles is everything! Raffles is London personified! A splendid fellow! But, as I said, the medals of the orders—no, even Raffles can't get at them."

The Lord of Westminster looked at the clock. "It's half past one, isn't it? Well, I pledge to steal all of the King's medals within twenty-four hours from now."

The peers opened their eyes and mouths. "But Lord, that's not funny," said the Earl of Westbury.

But the Lord of Westminster replied: "£50,000! Who is holding the bet?"

It was quiet for a moment. Fifty thousand pounds—that was a sum that had not ever been made, even in the Jockey Club. In the end, however, the gentlemen agreed that they would all come together—ten of them—to oppose the Lord of Westminster. He agreed.

"So £50,000 that I'm bringing you here the official King's medals in twenty-four hours," Lord Lister said.

At this moment a new gentleman took his place at the roulette table. "You have completely forgotten me, Lord," he said.

Raffles looked at him and saw Baxter's grim face. For seconds the two opponents measured each other across the table, while none of the gentlemen who sat next to them suspected that the two men were testing each other's strength at that moment.

It was the custom in the Jockey Club that every London gentleman could go in and out without being introduced. The club had broken with the rigid English manners, although it was the custom for a member of the club to introduce whoever was not a member. With a person as high as the Lord of Westminster it was ignored.

On the other hand, the appearance of the man who sat opposite the lord aroused some pity. His name had been overheard. In fact, Baxter had been careless enough to introduce himself to a servant as a police officer. So he did not call out the name of the newcomer aloud as usual.

In addition, Lord Lister, accustomed to moving himself in the narrowest circles of London, had the allure of a man of the world, while Baxter was far inferior to him in this respect. Yes, the presence of these gentlemen, with all their eyes set on him, confused the police inspector so much that he was about to get up to introduce himself in his official capacity when Raffles cut him off and said:

"Well, Count Pahlen, what are you betting against me?"

At the moment that the Lord of Westminster addressed the stranger as Count Pahlen, any doubts disappeared. The inspector regained his courage and determination not to continue a role, and, in order to avoid anything in front of Raffles, he replied: "I bet a million, Lord, that you cannot go ahead with your claim."

It was a great imprudence on the part of the inspector that he threw in a sum that no one believed in the fairytale existence of. A million pounds! No one of the Jockey Club would think that this Count Pahlen would bet a million. And at that moment, when the suspicion was awakened again, Raffles embracing the idea that his salvation was hanging by a thread said, turning to the inspector:

"I expected that you would pay such a sum! You are Raffles! It is of course easy for you to throw around such sums of money."

The effect of these words, which the real Raffles had spoken with the greatest calm of the world, was incredible. The club members reacted as if stung by tarantulas. Everything was viewed at a respectful distance, while at the same time the gazes of the gentlemen hung half-full of interest, half-disappointed about the supposed Raffles, Police Inspector Baxter.

He was uncomfortably numb. The master thief's move had come so unexpectedly that at first glance he couldn't find a word to gainsay him. At this moment Baxter was completely exposed.

Raffles used the silence silent to address the rest of the club members and said, "It is best to call a constable right away! This man is Raffles, I know him well."

A servant raced down the stairs to call the constable who had taken a post in the vestibule below. In the meantime, Baxter had found his way again. "It's a disgrace like no other," he shouted. Raffles is here!" He pointed to the Lord of Westminster, who responded with a contemptuous shrug of the accusation. But Baxter, caught in an indescribable rage, continued: "This is the worst thing you could have done, Raffles! You're under arrest! In the name of the law, you are under arrest!"

Baxter tried to assault the alleged Lord of Westminster who backed off from the inspector's punch and said, addressing the club members who had stepped aside in dismay: "We must tie up the madman if we don't want the name of this club to be compromised in all the newspapers tomorrow."

Meanwhile the servants had already rushed in to take sides with the Lord of Westminster, whose identity no one dared to doubt, and to bind the alleged master thief.

At that moment the patrolman entered.

"Constable," roared Baxter, "tell these gentlemen that the wretched man who calls himself Lord of Westminster is Raffles."

The constable looked at Lister, then at Baxter, and replied, waving at the inspector:

"But that's Raffles!"

That Baxter didn't have a stroke was astonishing. He was overpowered by the servants and dragged into an adjoining room, where the constable took care of him, because they wanted to get the supposed master thief out of the clubhouse without a ruckus.

The real Raffles turned to the rest of the gentlemen and

said: "I will go home because the interlude has upset me a bit! It is unbelievable that this rascal plays such a daring game even in the most distinguished clubs. Anyway our bet is on!"

The memory of this bet, which had already raised serious concerns among some club members, awoke the slumbering suspicion anew. And some remembered that the Lord of Westminster looked a bit like Raffles whose picture they had already seen in the newspapers. But when they had finally reached consensus with each other through speeches and counter-speeches and were looking for Raffles, by then the Lord of Westminster was gone. He had left the club building with six other members.

Several constables whom Baxter had ordered to follow him half an hour earlier came into the club. Now the little room where Baxter was held was unlocked. The constable who had taken Baxter to be Raffles had disappeared. It was none other than Charlie Brand who talked his friend out of the situation.

Filled with boundless anger, Baxter returned to Scotland Yard.

He understood that there was no way of dealing with this man with a large police force. He therefore decided to take over the guarding of the King's medals all by himself. This time, however, he refrained from having another reunion with Raffles. After Inspector Baxter had a long talk with the chancellor of the royal treasury, he hid in the lord's private office. This time Baxter had armed himself with a fully loaded Browning pistol and decided to shoot Raffles down if he dared carry out the daring robbery.

Baxter had told the Lord Chancellor the most incredible stories of the sophistication and audacity of John Raffles. He had discussed with the lord all the possible ways the Master Thief could get into the hidden vaults, where the medals were kept in a fireproof safe. The lord, convinced that Raffles would surely find an inventive way, had made the most extensive preparations. Yes, they had even thought of the overhead route and posted a constable on the roof of a nearby house.

Baxter had been crouched in his hiding place for twelve hours without seeing the slightest suspicious thing. The afternoon passed, the dusk came. A wonderful autumn night followed. The moon stood in the sky as clear as a golden lamp. Baxter was behind the heavy, purple-red doors that framed the large window, from which one had a clear view of the palace gardens. A water sprinkler was spurting monotonously out there. That was the only audible noise. The room was plush and elegantly decorated. There was a wolf's skin in front of the small desk, the furniture was purple and gold. A hand-held telephone was on the writing desk itself. A small ivory button protruded from the green cloth, like an electric bell. If one pressed on it, a secret door opened in the floor in front of the desk; this way you could get to the safe containing the medals. While Baxter crouched dead tired in his hiding place he regretted that only two hours remained from the time Raffles had to bring his bet to a close, While he himself suffered unspeakably from hunger and thirst and repeatedly examined the Browning anew and let his eyes slide around in the room flooded with moonlight, watching the Lord Chancellor's office he held two revolvers in front of him, ready to fire, and waited.

And Raffles, against whom the most incredible preparations had been made, chose the simplest way there was. At eleven o'clock in the morning the Lord Chancellor was informed of the visit of the Lord Chief Justice. That was nothing out of the ordinary. But the Lord Chancellor, not sure whether there was a trick behind this visit, stopped next to his table where the pistols were kept. The servant opened the door. An elegant, distinguished young man of about thirty entered, in impeccable, elegant black dress, the royal ribbon order under his left knee, the gold-trimmed gala hat in his left. He bowed, waited until the servant had closed the door behind him, took a few steps towards the Lord Chancellor and said: "My name is Raffles."

At first sight, the Lord Chancellor was so amazed by this boldness that he forgot to press the bell to call the servant. But instinctively he grabbed a revolver and held it up to the Great Unknown. He smiled, made a defensive movement with his hand, sat down on an armchair, put his hat on his knees and said:

"Please, your Excellency, put aside the shooting iron. I'm used to working without a revolver, and if I really do use it, I don't load it. You get along much more comfortably with your fellow men if you don't always rely on the revolver."

The Lord Chancellor, convinced that there was no way this man could harm him as long as he held him at such a distance, breathed a sigh of relief. He hoped to hold Raffles with him long enough for Baxter to come into his study of his own accord. Then it was easy to overpower the mysterious and scary man. Yes, it was uncanny that the Lord Chancellor couldn't help but feel a slight chill, while Lord Lister never lost his obliging smile.

With that, the master thief took out his golden case and held out his cigarettes to the Lord Chancellor. He was a passionate smoker himself; but he probably not would have made use of Raffles's kind offer, if it was up to him. But now he needed to stall, so the Lord Chancellor took one of the cigarettes, while every moment he looked at a door in fearful anticipation, the elegant gray of which stood out against the dark paneled wall.

"There is probably a secret entrance to the safe there, Excellency?" asked Raffles.

The Lord Chancellor, terrified that he had betrayed himself by his looks, replied:

"Oh no, not at all! Look for yourself! But now finally tell me what you want! You are Raffles! You are the Great Unknown! The most dangerous person of our century! So I want to draw your attention to the fact that I will shoot you down with the first movement you make."

But Lister just smiled. He took the cigarette, which he

had also taken out of the case, between his teeth and replied: "But the Queen can't light this for me, can she?" Raffles reached for the gold lighter that was on the desk next to the Lord Chancellor. But this proud man, fearful that Raffles could plan an attack on him, quickly took hold of it himself. He was getting more and more restless and nervous. Raffles's eager calm, his smile confused him completely. He no longer knew what to think of this behavior. So to be sure in any case he lit Raffles's cigarette himself and sat down in his chair again.

"Thank God," he thought after looking at the clock," the inspector can't be out much longer." Raffles smoked his cigarette in silence. The Lord Chancellor looked at him, also smoking, and the blue haze rose up to the ceiling; little clouds swirled around the heads of the men.

"A strange situation," thought the Lord Chancellor, who suddenly felt a dead tiredness. "Too weird! This Raffles is a character! He sits and stares at me and waits for Baxter to come and take him by the collar. Too weird!"

That was the last thing the Chancellor of the Exchequer thought. Then he fell asleep. The lit cigarette had slipped to the floor. Raffles put his ceremonial hat aside, picked up the cigarette, and tossed it in the ashtray. "She did her job," he muttered. "A dose of morphine in tobacco is the best soporific." He threw a smiling look at the Lord Chancellor, who was now really starting to snore, then he opened the desk, took the keys to the safe, stepped towards the entrance in the background of the room, pushed it aside, opened the secret door with a spring and disappeared into the dark corridor that led down to the vault.

One press of the electric flashlight Raffles carried and the path was brightly lit before him. After he had wandered through this seemingly endless corridor for about five minutes, which always went sloping downhill, and seemed to lead into the depths of the earth, a kind of casemate opened before his eyes, a large, square vault with a large safe in the middle in which the King's medals were housed.

Raffle's expressions never showed a moment of surprise or triumph. With that calm indifference that was the secret of all his successes, Raffles examined the box and then considered the possibility of success. It seemed difficult, almost impossible, to break open the heavy iron case with this poor lighting the electric flashlight discharged. Moreover, Raffles feared that he might be stopped if he left the palace on the route from which he had come. Surely it wasn't impossible that the numb man would wake up in the meantime before Raffles returned.

Then his gaze fell on a button that was just in front of the large safe on the floor.

Raffles understood.

The Lord Chancellor, of course, did not have to fall through the air to step into the vault when he had to reach the prize. So there was a connection between above and below, i.e. the iron safe could be pushed into the study above by engaging a spring. Raffles quickly pressed the button with his foot and instantly the trapdoor opened above him. At the same moment the safe started moving. A second trapdoor, which was attached under the floor on which the iron box stood, slid up on two rails attached to the walls and slowly pushed the heavy iron cabinet up with it. Raffles thought for a second. In the next moment he jumped next to the box. His right hand clung to the rear wall, he braced his feet against the steel walls, and so Raffles drove up from Hades to the surface of the earth, into the secret room in which Baxter earlier had lay in wait.

At the moment when the safe was on its best ground, the trapdoor closed again. Raffles pushed the safe back to the corner of the room so that the large glass door that led out into the magnificent garden was free. Then he set about breaking open this seemingly attack-proof locker in the same way as he had already done to Sir Woorman's.

There was a white star set in gold on a black ribbon, inside a golden crown and above it golden standards, helmet, armor and gun barrels bearing the Maltese Cross. Laughing, Raffles took out the glittering thing and stabbed his chest. Next to it he stuck the plain, not Indian, precious Danish Daneborg medal, the white cross with five golden crowns. Raffles held for a while in his right hand a red-blue crown with a white ring in the middle, which encircled a black eagle on an orange background.

Suum cuique "To each his own," he read on the Prussian Order of the Black Eagle.

"Hm. It actually works for me. 'To each his own,' that is also my motto."

Raffles hung around his neck the Greek Order of the Savior, a snow-white cross with a blue-rimmed gold ring in the middle and the image of Christ, carried by a gold crown and blue ribbon. There was fabulous flashing and glittering splendor: The Order of Saint Anne of Russia, a red cross with gold; the Teutonic Order, an elongated, black cross with a black ribbon; the massive, powerful Turkish Medjidie Order, a multi-shining, gray star with a gold plate and a red border over it and a crescent star and red-gold ribbon; also another example of the Order of the Garter, the blue loop with the golden cross and Saint George in the middle; the great British Order of Michael and George, a blunt star with a red cross, blue ribbon and the image of Saint Michael.

All, all the precious things, the splendid badges, the wonderful decorations of royal majesty, hung on Raffles's chest. A sea of embers and gold flickered and glittered together.

Finally Raffles took the last, most important medal in the world from the iron cabinet, the Austrian and Spanish Order of the Golden Fleece. Set in an ornamental gold structure, with a green background, hung under a multi-pointed red leaf under which also in gold was suspended the proud golden ram.

Slowly, with a mysterious smile, Raffles leaned on the ajar safe door. Then he stepped behind the desk and lit a cigarette. At that moment an electric light was turned on so that blinding glare filled the room. A dark figure in a white vest and white gloves had suddenly appeared in front of the desk. Baxter stood tall and lean in a black fur suit in front of Raffles and measured him with angry eyes.

Finally, the inspector whistled through his teeth. "Well, Raffles, the game is over once and for all! You are my prisoner!"

Raffles laughed as he took a few puffs from of his cigarette. Then Baxter tore the revolver out of his pocket in a rage, pointed it at Raffles and shouted in a thunderous voice: "Villain, don't you dare take a step! The first move you make I'll slam you down!"

The two men stood motionless, face to face, one clad in the insignia of golden splendor, unarmed, cheerful and calm; the other black and gloomy, threatening, flaming eyes pointing a gun at John Raffles, with which the slightest pressure would bring death.

There was a pause. The first to break the silence was the Master Thief:

"Tell me, dear Inspector, why you have to keep embarrassing yourself? Haven't you suffered enough? You will never achieve your goal, my arrest."

"See for yourself, Raffles," replied the policeman. "Whenever you want to, try to take it humorously. There is no way out for you. You can do what you want –the moment you strike the slightest chance to defend yourself, I'll shoot you down."

But Raffles was still laughing. "By thunder," he cried, "it's midnight; I have to be at the Jockey Club by half past one if I want to win my bet. "

"You won't win," the inspector shouted triumphantly.

"But I will."

"Never!"

"Watch!"

At that moment Raffles had stepped to the desk in a flash. Baxter pointed the revolver.

"Back up Raffles!"

"I'm never going back, Inspector, remember that!" he called and in the next moment pressed the button that protruded from the green desktop. Then the trapdoor opened noiselessly, which Inspector Baxter had never considered and which he stood on. He fell as fast as an arrow down into the black, yawning hole. At the same moment he threw his arms up involuntarily and shot, the inspector vanished into the depths of the vault.

"Hello, Captain Baxter, where did you go?" John Raffles laughed, taking his hand off the button. The trapdoor closed over the prisoner without a sound. The master thief smiled, then sat down at the desk and wrote the following down on a sheet of available paper:

"To His Excellency, the Lord Treasurer, H.M. Castle,

"In order to save your friend, Police Inspector Baxter, further unpleasant hours in the depths of the safe, I inform you that he had to go there in order not to prevent me from carrying out my plan. So, open the cellar and give Baxter his freedom.

"Your devoted,

"John Raffles"

Then he put on his ceremonial hat, left the room through the large glass door, walked through the garden and swung himself over the high wall surrounding the royal castle's park, just as the Lord Chancellor awoke and sounded the alarm.

Chapter V

The Mysterious Coupé

Lord Lister called a passing cab. The coachman waved the whip in greeting in front of the elegant gentleman, whose glittering medals shimmered through the half-open cloak.

"Jockey Club. St. James Street."

The horse pulled in and quickly reached its goal. Those who had bet against the Lord of Westminster, who had so suddenly turned out to be Raffles, sat in the high, elegant club hall. Actually, no one really thought of this sensational adventure anymore when suddenly the door opened and an elegant,

distinguished young man, whose coat the servant had taken off
in the anteroom, stepped in.

Had they not already been astonished by the distinction
of his appearance and by the elegant facial features, the flicker
and glitter of the medals, this flood of light and brilliance alone
was enough to captivate the eyes of all the gentlemen on the new
guest.

And like wildfire it went from mouth to mouth:

"Raffles!"

The Master Thief bowed, laughing, to the Earl of
Westbury, who, with his mouth wide open, looked petrified at
the man who had entered, whom he had never believed to see
again. There was dead silence in the hall, only interrupted by the
exclaiming of astonishment and the amazement of the members.

Lord Rothsborne clamped his monocle.

"My goodness! Is it really you! You have—but that is
not even possible."

Lord Lister was still smiling. He stepped from one of the
club members to the other and said:

"Verify, gentlemen, that I have won my bet."

Shaking their heads they looked at the gold medals, now
at Raffles, who was standing in front of them, lovable, elegant
and chic as always, his hands lightly against the table top.

They had to convince themselves that the medals were
genuine and complete. Not one of them was fake! Everybody
understood that.

"If I were not a modern person, I would believe in magic," said the Earl of Westbury.

But Lord Rothsborne added: "We lost our bet."

Nobody contradicted. The members of the Jockey Club were gentlemen. John Raffles, the master thief, was standing in front of them, the man whom the whole of the London police were after, like the pack stalking deer. But they had lost their bet.

And so they didn't say another word, instead they took out a billfold and paid the required sum.

"*Merci*, gentlemen," said Raffles without removing the smile on his face, folded the bills and stuck them in his breast pocket. "And now you have to send those the good, glittering things back to the treasury again."

The Master Thief carefully removed the medals, piece by piece, and handed them to the Earl of Westbury. Then he left.

His cab was still waiting downstairs.

He mentioned a street near his apartment that no one in London knew. Once there, he sent the cab away, went inside and exchanged a few words with Charlie Brand, who was waiting for him.

He laughed when Lord Lister told him about his experience. Then he disappeared into the next room, changed his clothes, came back as an elegant London coachman, then went down into the stable, harnessed the horse himself and brought to the front the carriage that Raffles had bought a few weeks earlier.

The Great Unknown got in. "Bromley Burdett Road, Charlie."

"All right," he replied, and let the whip dance over the horse's back.

As Raffles drove towards the beautiful Miss Ellen Crofton's apartment, the club members had recovered from the numbness into which the appearance of Raffles had put them. They agreed that it would be better if the police would get the money back from Raffles and return it to them. The Earl of Westbury rose with dignity, went to the phone, and informed Scotland Yard that Raffles had just been to the Jockey Club.

Shortly after he made his call that Baxter got there. It was no longer an empty phrase for the inspector when he said Raffles was driving him crazy. He was half-mad from anger and pain. No sooner had he received the telephone message from the Earl of Westbury than he ordered five constables to follow him on his bike, even though he was dead tired and could hardly stand on his feet.

He swung himself onto his bicycle and the six policemen chased through the darkness like ghosts at night.

##

Colonel Crofton and his family lived in a small house that consisted of four rooms. He was a resilient man despite his fifty years of age, but a severe wound forced him to walk with a cane.

At the moment when Lord Lister was about to press the

bell in front of the apartment door, a crackling, violent voice reached his ear.

"And I tell you, Colonel, Sir Woorman won't credit you for a day! Even if he is in prison, his principles remain the same! You know that I am his agent! I'll foreclose tomorrow if you don't pay today."

Raffles withdrew the hand that was already on the bell.

"But I will explain to you that it is impossible for me to fulfill my obligations today," said a deep, honorable voice. "Sir Woorman made me certain promises. I will use all my strength to—"

"Poppycock," threw out the other crudely," "pay or get out."

There was a pause, then the cracking voice began again: "Sir Woorman, incidentally, would be inclined to hold off if you were ready to do him a favor.

"If it goes with my honor he can pay me," said Crofton.

"Oh, put aside the honor and such nonsense," said the negotiator. "Miss Ellen, your daughter, will be questioned as a witness tomorrow. Three-quarters of the fate of Sir Woorman will depend on her statement. The gentleman expects the lady to be silent. She is the only witness as to what went on in the Band Men's club who could be got hold of. Everyone else escaped, thank God. So, if the lady disguises the facts a little, embellishes a little, things are much better for Sir Woorman. In that case, he would be willing to—"

At this moment the bell rang. A slight step of the girl was heard.

Raffles saw Miss Ellen's pale countenance, moistened with tears. She looked at him with wide, puzzled eyes. Then a bright light flew over her face.

"Father! Father!" she exclaimed in a tone of joyful astonishment. "It's him! It is the Lord whom I have twice to thank for salving my honor."

Lord Lister stepped out of the hallway into the light that poured through the open door of one of the rooms. He was facing the Colonel, who hurried up to him and cordially extended the right hand. Raffles pressed the offered hand, but at the same time fended off the words of thanks that were already floating on the lips of the brave former officer.

Then he turned to the stranger who had fixed himself in the hallway. It was an unpleasant person who smelled of booze and, despite the obtrusively elegant clothing, could not deny his disgrace. The bulldog face betrayed an Irishman, the eyes, which had the stupid expression of the drinker, welled out of their sockets.

With a look of surprise, horror, and anger all at once, he stared at Raffles.

"Who are you and what are you doing here?" He asked, burying his left hand in his pocket where his wallet was hidden. "My name is Fred Campbell. I am Sir Woorman's agent."

"You have a nice job there," said Lord Lister

sardonically.

"Sir," roared the other, "how dare you—

The Master Thief smiled contemptuously.

"Don't go out of your way, Mr. Campbell, to intimidate me. You won't like it! It's bad enough you're an agent for an already half-convicted murderer and professional bandit."

"You are crazy!" shouted Mr. Campbell, pulling the sleeve off his right arm. "Look at these muscles. Want me to punch your nose off your face?"

Lady Ellen was about to jump between the men, but at a speed that no one could have foreseen, John Raffles had struck the braggart with his fist under the chin so that it flew back like a rubber ball. He muttered several Irish curses, but dared not attack this slender, elegant man who had the tendons and muscles of a giant.

"What do you want from me?" he stammered.

"First I wanted to teach you a lesson so that in the future you would know how to behave towards decent, honorable people," Lord Lister said, by pointing with his hand to the Colonel and his daughter. "You should be glad, Mr. Campbell, that a man who has shed his blood for England in India will receive such sentiments as you and your employer even in his apartment. As far as the testimony of this lady is concerned, she will tell the truth under all circumstances, because Lady Crofton would be really nasty if she wanted to become a liar because of a villain.

"She will testify that she was ambushed, knocked out and dragged to St. James Street by the goofy band club members. Sir Woorman will then be comfortable to name his accomplices, who for the most part are made up of depraved offspring of the *jeunesse dorée* and who have known the worthy companions of the crimes of the noble Sir Woorman."

"Then Colonel Crofton will be a beggar tomorrow," Campbell hissed.

"That won't be the case either," continued John Raffles with a laugh. "The Colonel will continue his business as before. On the contrary! He will renounce his previous financier once and for all, for it is utterly unworthy of an English officer and gentleman to work with a villain like Sir Woorman."

After these words, which astonished each of the three persons in no small way, the Great Unknown reached into his pocket and snatched the receipt from Campbell's hand. "How much is the Colonel's debt?" he asked harshly.

Campbell didn't know what to do. "Two hundred pounds this time, and 475 pounds from before," he said softly.

"That makes six hundred and seventy-five pounds together," Raffles said. "Here is the sum.

"But—" the other began.

Raffles pointed to the open corridor door that led to the stairwell. "Don't say a word further, Mr. Campbell, if you don't want to get out of this house sooner than you think."

With hunched shoulders and squinting eyes, shy as a

dog, Mr. Campbell the negotiator crept out.

With both hands the Colonel seized the right hand of the Master Thief, of whom he knew nothing more than that he was as much the enemy of the London villains as he was of Scotland Yard.

"How can I ever thank you?" he slurred.

"Your respect is enough for me," said Lord Lister simply. Then his gaze fell on Lady Ellen, who, completely absorbed in his sight, shyly and hesitantly stretched out her hand to him, as if she did not dare to pay him her thanks. He did not take hers to thank him. He took her little delicate cheek and put it to his lips.

"Can I - ever - serve you?" she asked softly, uttering every word, lowering her gaze to the floor.

He stared at her for a moment, with a dark smile, while flaming red covered her cheeks.

"Maybe," he replied. Your tears, lady, are thanks enough for me."

"And who - whom should I properly include in my prayer?" she asked hesitantly, opening her eyes to him.

He shook his head seriously.

"Don't ask who I am, lady. I am happiness and fatality in one person."

Speaking like this, he bowed and left this house, into which he had suddenly stepped like sunshine, without giving time to those whose happiness he helped with to come to their senses.

The outlines of his carriage rose gray and hazy from the fog of the night.

"37 Westend Street," Raffles ordered loudly. At that moment, Charlie Brand leaned slightly from the box and whispered:

"Inspector Baxter is here with five cops. They're hiding."

Raffles nodded, chuckling a hearty laugh from his mouth.

"Drive on, coachman."

The coupé closed and the car began moving towards Westend Street.

At the same time, five figures riding bicycles emerged from the fog. They swung up on their steel horses and raced to either side of the car, keeping a close eye on the lanterns on the jockey box, so that it was impossible for John Raffles to leave car by the left or right.

After a sharp drive of nearly three quarters of an hour, while Baxter and his five companions nearly contracted pulmonary consumption, the car stopped at its destination. Baxter raised his arm and ordered his companions to jump off the bikes and circle the car.

"We'll stop him before he goes upstairs," he ordered. "Maybe we'll catch some of his accomplices that way."

It had been Inspector Baxter's brilliant idea to go to

Bromley. Indeed, despite the defeats he had, he was not an underestimated opponent and at least Raffles's most dangerous enemy. Baxter had remembered the scene in Scotland Yard when the Master Thief, who was then posing as Constable White, was so conspicuously protecting a young lady. The inspector recalled that he had saved this lady back in the Band Men's club and that she was a main witness against Sir Woorman. Since he already knew from the practice of the Great Unknown that he would seek out those who had suffered from an injustice, Baxter had smartly found the right lead this time. He was not a little happy. This time Raffles shouldn't get away from him. This time, the shot he held ready for the one who had so often outwitted and defeated him should not go wrong. This time.

"But it's a long time coming, Inspector," said one of the constables. Baxter was getting impatient too. He waited a while, then with a ready-to-fire revolver he went to the door of the coupé, opened it and said:

"Get out, Raffles, you are under arrest."

But Raffles didn't come, and Baxter saw that the car was empty. With a curse, he staggered back.

"Coachman!"

"Yes, Inspector?"

"Where's Raffles?"

Charlie Brand laughed so hard that it could be heard down the street.

"You want to know if I know where Raffles is? I never

heard that before! Am I Inspector Baxter? He always knows where Raffles is."

"Save your jokes. Your passenger was Raffles."

"My passenger? Excuse me, Inspector, but that is a big mistake. My passenger was the famous magician Ben Akiba, who will soon be holding a big soirée in London."

Baxter hit the horse with his knuckle. "I'll have you arrested if you keep it up."

But Charlie insisted that it was none of his business and that Ben Akiba had already made such jokes by making himself invisible.

"Maybe," he added with a laugh, "Raffles also knows how to make himself invisible."

The inspector, foaming with rage, took Charlie Brand to Scotland Yard with the wagon. But after a short interrogation he was released because Charlie had excellent recommendations and was able to prove that a few days ago he had entered the service of the Lord of Westminster as a coachman.

"But that Lord of Westminster is Raffles," the inspector shouted angrily.

"Really?" replied Charlie. "That's good to know. Ai, ai! Look! The Lord of Westminster is Raffles. Yeah, you can't blame me for not recognizing and catching Raffles, can you? That's your job, Inspector. So, I wish you the best of luck and hope that you will let me recover now."

What could Baxter do? He had to let the supposed

coachman go without knowing that Charlie was Raffles's secretary.

Halfway through his comfortable drive home Charlie stopped the horse, dismounted, and looked in the coupé. "Yeah, lucky they didn't examine the car," he muttered. "They always forget the trees for the forest. If the brave inspector had looked closely at the interior, he would have undoubtedly noticed a sliding floor."

And Raffles? As soon as the car had been in motion for ten minutes, he had pushed the floor aside and let himself slide unhurriedly between the wheels. Then he jumped up and cleaned his clothes while the coupé vanished into the fog of the night with the policeman in pursuit.

He raised his manicured hand in greeting: "*Adieu*, Inspector Baxter! *Auf fröhliches Weidersehen*! Good bye!"

With these words he went to a bar.

THE END

Coming soon:

Lord Lister 4: The Coffin's Treasure

Joseph A. Lovece is a retired journalist, and collector of dime novels, pulp magazines and comic books. He lives in Ormond Beach, Florida.